WYOMING BLOOD FEUD

Neither Rafe Charnley nor his son Jeff could have foreseen how quickly their family tensions would escalate when Jeff falls in love with the daughter of the sheepherders with whom the family have a long-standing feud. Rafe cannot see his son's actions as anything but a deeply personal betrayal. Jeff is desperate to prove his feelings to his father — but when his beau's brother is accused of violating a land boundary, Rafe threatens to have him strung up. Can the hostilities between them be rectified without blood being spilled?

DALE GRAHAM

WYOMING BLOOD FEUD

Complete and Unabridged

LINFORD
Leicester

First published in Great Britain in 2015 by
Robert Hale Limited
London

First Linford Edition
published 2018
by arrangement with
Robert Hale
an imprint of
The Crowood Press
Wiltshire

A catalogue record for this book is available
from the British Library.

ISBN 978–1–4448–3592–2

Published by
F. A. Thorpe (Publishing)
Anstey, Leicestershire

Set by Words & Graphics Ltd.
Anstey, Leicestershire
Printed and bound in Great Britain by
T. J. International Ltd., Padstow, Cornwall

This book is printed on acid-free paper

Foreword

If there was one thing likely to incense the cattlemen of the old West, then the encroachment of sheep on to their ranges was top of the list. There was no law to prevent the grazing of woollies. But ranchers had an inborn hatred of these odious beasts. Indeed some refused to eat mutton, or wear wool next to their skin. Sodbusters came a close second. But sheep were regarded as the devil's spawn.

The claim that woollies secreted a glandular fluid the smell of which repelled cattle was false, though widely believed at the time. Another myth was that they could spoil grassland simply by walking across it. Sheep did, however, chew the grass down to its roots and could ruin pasturage with their sharp hoofs.

The coming of the large white herds represented a theft of the land that the cattlemen regarded as their rightful property. But sheep offered poorer folk the chance to prosper. They had the advantage of being more docile than cattle and could be easily controlled by a couple of men with a dog. It was perhaps inevitable that their expansion was in terrain less accessible to the longhorns.

Only towards the end of the nineteenth century was it finally acknowledged that cattle and sheep could in fact coexist.

It is no surprise, therefore, that violence frequently erupted between the two factions. Many sheepherders were immigrants from Europe. The cattlemen regarded these invaders, both the animals and their herders, as inferior beings and many vigilante groups were formed to patrol the ranges.

'Deadlines' were laid down beyond which any herder was liable to be severely beaten. Some were even strung up as a warning to others who sought to invade the territories where cattle-rearing was king.

Any sheep found were often killed.

Rim-rocking was a common practice, where sheep were driven over a nearby cliff.

One infamous feud in Arizona between the cattle-raising Grahams and the Tewkesbury sheepmen was carried on relentlessly for fifteen years. It only ended when the last of the Tewkesbury men was shot down.

But feuds over sheep were not only between opposing groups. Incidents sometimes occurred that blew up into sweeping confrontations within families. One such tragedy took place in Wyoming between a father and son.

1

Cattle King

Rafe Charnley sat his horse atop a hill overlooking the Big Horn valley. A wide-brimmed black Stetson shaded out the noonday sun. He leaned over the head of the equally black Arab stallion, surveying the grazing cattle below. A sigh of satisfaction trickled from between lips gripping a large cigar. As far as the eye could see, this was his land, fought over and nurtured this last twenty years since he had brought the first herd up the Goodnight-Loving trail from Texas.

Stretching his arms out like a prophet giving thanks to the good Lord, he nodded to his companion.

'It makes a guy feel mighty good inside, Curly,' he opined with feeling. 'Knowing that all this belongs to me.'

Unlike Curly Bob Spendler, the

ranch owner always wore a black suit and necktie, even on a hot summer's day like this one. It was a feature that he liked to think marked him out as a successful businessman. The foreman preferred the rough working garb of a range hand. He had no posturing pretensions like the boss.

But that did not mean he disdained Charnley. A strong degree of respect existed between the two old comrades. Each knew and relied upon their mutual strengths and abilities. It was a tight bond that had made the Flying Arrow the pre-eminent spread in the territory.

Friends as well as working colleagues, the two men had been inseparable from the beginning. They had ridden together during the war. Once the bitter conflict had staggered to a close, it seemed natural for the two buddies to drift down to Texas. There they had punched cows and gone up the trails to the Kansas railheads. Hallooing and roistering was a much enjoyed pursuit once they had been paid off.

That was until Rafe finally decided it was time to settle down.

Hard work and the innate ability to help his employers negotiate a good deal from sharp-eyed cattle buyers had given Charnley the wherewithal to buy his own spread. Prosperity had quickly followed. A fervent yearning to own the biggest outfit in the West was an ambition verging on the obsessive that drove the cattleman. And Curly Bob was always there in support.

Both men had even courted the same girl. Bob held no simmering resentments that Lisa May Starkey had chosen the more dynamic of the two. Curly Bob had been at Rafe's side as best man for their wedding. A far greater degree of backing was needed when they had buried Lisa May following a bout of fever two years previously.

Curly Bob was content just to take a back seat and go with the flow. Now the foreman of Rafe Charnley's Flying Arrow outfit, he shared the rancher's avid glow of satisfaction of a job well done.

Theirs was now the biggest spread in Wyoming territory. Not a strip of barbed wire was in sight. Free range was how they liked it. No chopping up of land to impede the natural movement of cattle across the rolling expanse of grassland. Since its invention in 1873 as a cost-effective replacement for wooden fencing, more and more land had become sectioned off. Dirt farmers were often the principal culprits.

'You're right there, boss,' Curly Bob concurred, accepting a cigar and lighting up. 'Let's hope we can keep it this way.'

The hint of concern for the future was evident in the foreman's tone and it was picked up by Charnley.

'That's why we always have to be on guard and deal ruthlessly with predators,' he avowed gruffly. It was clear to them both that he was not referring to coyotes and buzzards. Nor even the despised sodbusters.

Another growing and far more serious problem troubling the rancher was the steady influx of sheep herds. Two had been broken up and driven off since the spring thaw.

Rafe was adamant that no sheep would encroach on any of his land. He hoped that the abrupt, decisive treatment meted out would discourage any further incursions of the detested beasts. Notices along the boundaries of his holding left culprits in no doubt as to the penalty that would ensue should the warnings be ignored.

Rafe was scanning the activities of the men down below who had welcomed the extra pay to work overtime. It was Sunday so most of the hands would be sleeping off the previous night's excesses in the bunkhouse. It was round-up time, which was one of the busiest periods in the ranching calendar. New calves were being brought in off the range for branding with the distinctive Flying Arrow mark.

Any strays from other outfits were also rounded up and penned in ready for collection. It was a system that had worked well since the cattle industry had come to Wyoming. All the spreads cooperated with one another to ensure fair play was adhered to.

Only two men were conspicuous by their laxity. Lounging idly beside a pitch-pole fence, they casually watched as the regular hands laboured at their tasks under the hot sun. Curly Bob gave a snort of disdain on spotting the figures of Snag LaBone and his buddy Skinner Gillette.

'Those two guys give me the creeps, boss,' he grumbled, pointing a finger at the arrogant loafers. 'You sure we need shirkers like them on the payroll?'

Only Bob Spendler could address the boss in such a boldly incisive manner. Even the rancher's son would have hesitated to challenge his father's decisions.

'You know why they were taken on, Curly.' Charnley shook his head. Doubts had been expressed by the foreman previously about the hiring of gunslingers. 'You still harping on about how we dealt with those land-grabbers last year? We needed their kind of help then. You have to admit that.'

Spendler's nose wrinkled. But he remained close-lipped.

'And we need 'em now even more so,' Charnley continued, 'with all these sheep dippers pressing their claim to Flying Arrow land. Those hardasses have the wherewithal to discourage them. LaBone and his sidekick don't come cheap. But they were highly recommended by Sirus Windsock.'

The owner of the Yellow Dog, the largest saloon in Casper, was another dude who was decidedly suspect when it came to bending the law to suit his own devious schemes. But Curly knew better than to voice any further objections to Rafe Charnley's choice of associates. That would drive a wedge into the harmonious affiliation that he had no wish to jeopardize.

There was only so much dissension the boss would tolerate. Curly was a special friend, but there were limits. The Texas rancher was well known for his caustic temper. He could display a ruthless streak when dealing with those who were disloyal, as those land-grabbers had discovered to their cost.

Only the previous month a horse-thief had been strung up and left to dangle on the main road into Casper: a brutal yet accepted method of dealing with such lawbreakers. The local sheriff had even commended Rafe's resolute action. Charnley's eye roved across the various groups down below.

'Can't spot Jeff down there,' he remarked, his narrowed gaze flitting over the various riders gathering in the animals for branding. A stern expression clouded the rancher's visage. He expected his son to provide a good example to the other hands. 'He's meant to be supervising the cutting out. You got any notion as to where he is, Curly?'

The foreman shrugged, although he suspected where young Jeff was probably hanging out.

'He might have gone off to see some

gal he met at the hoedown in Chuck Yancey's barn last week,' came the hesitant reply as Curly struggled to conceal a smile. 'He's been talking about her all week.'

'She ain't one of Heggerty's new brood, is she?'

Another cautious lift of the shoulders from Spendler. Fats Heggerty ran another of Casper's dens of iniquity. A man who was big in all the wrong places, he was well known for the lusty dames he brought in from the bigger towns of Cheyenne and Denver.

Rafe huffed some. He harboured no objections to his son seeking female company, but there were limits. Saloon dames certainly did not fit with his plans for the boy. In truth he wanted his son to find a good wife to curb his wayward spirit, to settle him down. Rafe wasn't getting any younger. Some time in the near future he would need to hand over the reins and enjoy his retirement.

'It better not be some saloon gal.

Those floozies will be all over Jeff like a rash. He's a good catch for any dame.'

'I'm sure he'll choose the right one when the time is right,' Curly assured him. 'Jeff knows which side his bread's buttered.'

Had the foreman known the real identity of Jeff's female interest he would not have been so nonchalant in his response. Young Charnley had deliberately laid a false trail to conceal his true intentions. His father continued to air his thoughts for the boy's matrimonial prospects.

'He could do worse than court one of the Yancey sisters. They're from good ranching stock. Either one of them gals would make the perfect wife for Jeff if only he'd show some interest in them.' He slapped his thigh in frustration. 'What's wrong with the boy?'

Curly knew exactly why young Charnley had spurned the coquettish flirting attempted by Maud Yancey in particular. He hawked out a scornful guffaw. 'You must be joking, Rafe.

Those two dames are as plain as the open prairie and you know it. Jeff wants somebody to light his fire and curdle his loins.'

Rafe Charnley's moustache twitched with acerbic disapproval at his friend's jocular comment. He agreed wholeheartedly with his buddy's waspish comment. But that wasn't the point, as he forcefully retorted.

'All I want for my son is a woman who can produce a male offspring to inherit the Charnley kingdom and keep the Flying Arrow at the head of the pack. Is that so goldarned bad? If'n the boy wants to spread his wings after he's married, then that's his affair.'

A rather unfortunate choice of words that elicited a wry guffaw from his foreman.

★   ★   ★

The young man in question was at that very moment splayed out beneath the swaying boughs of a cottonwood in the adjoining valley. An exceedingly pretty girl of a similar age was tickling him with a piece of grass. The two young lovers were enjoying a picnic, although their doe-eyed regard for each other was getting far more attention than the fried chicken and freshly baked biscuits.

Jeff grabbed the girl and drew her down beside him. They kissed. It was a long and passionate moment that seemed to last for ever. Jeff's loins were tingling, the blood pounding in his head when the girl wriggled out of his grasp. A sigh of frustration hissed from his open mouth. As always he wanted to take the amorous contact further.

Elsa Fallenborg would also have loved nothing more than to surrender her virtue to this handsome rancher. But she was well aware of the complications that might well arise should things go wrong. Anyway, a girl needed to remain chaste and pure for her husband. Elsa was no doxy. She had her self-respect and knew full well that 'tainted goods' were reviled by most men seeking a wife.

They had only been walking out for two months; theirs was a liaison that could only be carried on incognito. For Elsa was the daughter of an immigrant sheepherder of Swedish descent. Her classic Scandinavian looks incorporated flowing blond locks and a lithe figure. Unlike the calico queens, she possessed a natural beauty that even a small amount of face paint would have marred.

Jeff had been instantly smitten the moment he set eyes on her at one of Yancey's barn dances. But should either of their parents ever discover the illicit secret, all hell would break loose. Prudence and rationality decreed that their ill-fated tryst had to be conducted in secret. They refused to acknowledge that their conflicting backgrounds meant that any chance of a happy future was inevitably doomed from the start.

Jeff and Elsa were in love. Hope springs eternal in the human breast. Prayers that some miracle would intervene to bless their union were offered up every day.

17

Firmly, Elsa removed his searching hands from around her body, her pert nose twitching in feigned annoyance as she coyly declared:

'Not until our relationship is on a more solid footing. After all, a girl has her reputation to consider.' The long eyelashes fluttered suggestively, which did not help.

'But a guy has his . . . needs, Elsa,' the young man whined, hoping to win her round yet secretly respecting her beliefs.

'What you need is a cold bath to cool you down,' she chuckled with a teasing lift of the shoulders. Then she straightened her dress and stood up. When this stage was reached in their meetings, she knew it was time to call it a day.

Reluctantly, Jeff accepted that his libido would need to be reined in for yet another week. It was tough on a hot-blooded young man. He sighed and set his hat atop his thatch of brown wavy hair.

'Same time next week, then?'

The girl's mouth turned up in a flirtatious pout. She flicked her long golden hair back. 'Maybe. It all depends if'n I still want to be wooed by a rough cowboy like you, doesn't it?' Then she mounted up. A meaningful wink conveyed more than any words could ever express as she spurred off.

They both knew she would be there, under the same cottonwood, waiting and eager at the appointed hour for his strong arms to encircle her trim waist.

Jeff watched as his beloved rode away. He waited until she had disappeared over the crest of Spyglass Hill into the neighbouring valley before mounting his own horse. An hour later he crested the southern foothills before descending into the valley of Big Horn River.

It was Curly Bob who spotted the plume of rising dust over on the northern rim.

'Looks like we got company, boss,' he remarked. As the rider drew closer the Texas high crown favoured by Jeff Charnley became instantly recognizable. 'It's

Jeff. Now I wonder what he's been up to?'

A smile crossed the foreman's leathery features. He suspected that the young man was not returning from a viewing of the prized bull they were intent on procuring from Chuck Yancey of the Box Y. Rafe, however, was not so accepting of his son's unwarranted absence from the ranch. The expression on his face hovered between a barely suppressed scowl and downright anger.

The two men nudged their horses down the boulder-strewn slope, twisting between stands of blackthorn and juniper bushes.

'Howdie there, you guys!' Jeff called out. The breezy greeting elicited a welcoming return wave from Curly Bob. 'Sorry I'm a bit late arriving. I had some . . . erm . . . personal business that needed sorting in town.'

A smirking guffaw from the foreman caused Jeff's face to blossom into ocotillo red. Rafe Charnley came directly to the point.

'Where in thunder have you been, boy?' He didn't wait for a reply to the irate query. 'These guys have been working their butts off doing your work.'

'Give the kid a break, boss,' interjected Curly. 'He ain't been gone that long.'

'You keep out of this, Curly,' snapped Charnley as the atmosphere rapidly sank to a biting chill. Thinking about his son's contrary lifestyle had made the tough rancher increasingly tetchy. 'This is between me and him.'

The stern rebuke caught Curly off guard. He was too stunned to issue a reply. He had never seen Rafe this mad before. The guy had gotten himself into a right stew. And for what? His son's cavorting with some gal of whom he didn't approve?

The miffed foreman was given no further time to mull over the implications of the sudden flare-up.

'Your place is here,' Charnley railed, shaking his fist. 'This is our busiest time of the year as you well know. Yet all you can do is go off cavorting with some tart of a saloon chickadee.' Rafe was now in full flow, his face the colour of a ripe plum.

But unlike the visibly cowed Curly Bob Spendler, young Charnley was not about to be upbraided in front of the hired hands without a spirited response.

'I ain't no kid any more, Pa. And I sure as hell won't stand by and get pushed around by you or anyone else. What I do in my own time is no business of yourn. The sooner you understand that — '

'How dare you speak to me in that manner, you insolent young pup.' Rafe pushed his horse forward. 'I'm your father and you'll do as I say.' The quirt in his hand was all set to deliver a blow when two men rode into the work camp.

'Hey boss,' yelled one of the cowboys. 'Lookee here what we done found.'

The imminent fracas between father and son was temporarily halted as everybody turned to see what the line rider called Jackie Blue and his partner had brought in. Even a couple of watching jackdaws turned to follow the sudden interruption.

'We'll talk about this later, Jeff . . . in private.' Rafe Charnley slung a final glower at his recalcitrant offspring. Then he swung to see what all the commotion was about.

'What you got there, Blue?' he asked the line rider.

2

Bad Blood

'Me and Jupe have caught us a real live sheep-shafter, Mr Charnley,' Jackie Blue burbled excitedly. To emphasize this dubious good fortune, he planted his boot heel into the victim's back and drove him forward.

The guy, who was naught but a boy, lurched and stumbled. His hands were tied. Unable to maintain his balance, the young sheepherder fell to his knees. His face was smeared with dried blood. The two cowpokes had clearly given him a going-over before driving him back to camp on foot like a maverick steer.

Already steamed up, the arrival of a sheepman only served to exacerbate the rancher's bad mood.

'By glory! You fellas better have a good reason for dragging some mangy sheep-dipper on to my ranch.'

'We found him over on the north range pushing a herd of those durned critters towards our best grass,' Jupe Kemple explained. 'The rat claimed he was collecting loose woollies that had strayed across the boundary line.'

'Jupe and me reckoned you'd want to know about it,' Jackie added.

'Its true,' the young sheepman butted in. 'They escaped from the main herd after the thunderstorm yesterday. I was only collecting them to drive back on to our land.'

Rafe was not listening. As far as he was concerned, any altercation involving sheep would receive short shrift. These lowlife trespassers needed to be shown that there was no room for sheep in Wyoming. As leader of the local Cattlemen's Association, the boss of Flying Arrow took his responsibilities seriously.

There was only one way to deal with scum like this. Hang them. But maybe there was a better way.

'Now that I know what happened,

I'm glad my boys didn't string up this piece of dung.' Eyes burning with hate bore into the quaking youngster. A jabbing finger laid emphasis to his every word. 'Its lucky for you that I'm in a good mood today. So I'm letting you go to carry a message. You tell those scum over yonder hill that your dirt-grubbing kind are not welcome around here. And you make darned sure they know that this is the final warning. Ignore it and we'll come over and burn you out.'

'Don't waste your time with this varmint, Mr Charnley.' Snag LaBone shouldered aside the ring of gaping cowhands and now proceeded to issue his own threat. 'The only law these sidewinders understand is gun law.' The hard-boiled tough drew his revolver and snapped back the hammer to full cock. 'Just say the word and one more sheep-dipper hits the high trail. Sending him back strapped to a saddle horse with a bullet in his guts will be a far more powerful message. One they can't ignore.'

'Maybe you're right there, Snag,' agreed the ranch boss. 'The time for talk is over. These guys need teaching a lesson they'll not forget.' He nodded for the hired gunman to do his worst.

Jeff Charnley had heard enough. He leapt off his horse and grabbed hold of LaBone's gun hand. The weapon exploded. But the bullet went high and wide. The two men struggled as LaBone growled out a savage curse. Jeff managed to wrench the gun from his hand and toss it aside out of reach. Then he dived on to the fallen tough.

But LaBone was a cunning brawler and twisted away. He leapt to his feet and replied with a couple of sharp jabs that drove Jeff back. Blood poured from a split lip. The circle of cowboys widened to give the fighters more room.

A good set-to was always something to enjoy. Most of those present were no fans of the hired gunman. But neither were they supporters of any sheep-herder.

The tussle raged on as punches were

exchanged and blocked. Both men were breathing hard, sucking air into tortured lungs. But Jeff was beginning to get the upper hand. That was when LaBone showed his devious side by drawing a throwing-knife from a boot sheath. A swift overarm throw would have been impossible to avoid. Jeff stood no chance if the lethal blade was launched.

'Nobody gets the better of Snag LaBone,' growled the incensed braggart.

A shot rang out before the knife could go winging on its fatal course. The bullet was accurately placed. It struck the hilt of the blade, smashing it into a myriad fragments.

'Aaaaagh! That's my gun hand,' the tough yelled as the bullet tore a hole in his hand. He fell to the ground as blood poured from the punctured appendage.

'The next one will be through your head.' Curly Bob held his own revolver steady as a rock. Smoke trailed from the barrel. 'So don't try any more sneaky tricks.'

Lurking on the edge of the gathering, Skinner Gillette decided to take charge. His gun rose. It was aimed at the boss's son.

Only Jeff Charnley's swift and timely intervention had saved the sheepherder from being cut down. Here was his chance to repay the solicitous act.

'Look out!' the young man shouted.

Jeff's reaction was instantaneous. He threw himself to one side and drew his own pistol. The gun barked. Two slugs ploughed into Gillette, finishing him off. In the space of a brief second it was all over. Everybody just stared at the dead man and his injured colleague.

The sudden outpouring of violence had taken them all by surprise. Everybody present was momentarily stunned at what had happened. Jeff was well aware that if he had not stepped in the dire situation could have easily rampaged out of control.

How had it come to this? That was the thought raging inside Jeff Charnley's brain. Only an hour before he had been in seventh heaven courting his girl. Now he had been forced into killing a man. He quickly threw off the anguish threatening to churn his guts to mush.

With slow deliberation he turned to face his father.

'This is all your fault,' he spat out. The biting accusation was emphasized by an admonitory finger pointed at his father. 'You and your blinkered hatred of anything that don't produce beef has turned you into a mindless bigot. And now you've turned me into a killer as well.'

Rafe Charnley was not about to accept such an angry remonstration from his own kin. Especially not in front of the hired hands. Saving face was essential to maintain his authority.

'You stupid boy,' the irate rancher hollered back. 'Do you realize what you're saying, standing up for these dirty sheep tramps? If'n this gets out, I'll be the laughing stock of the territory. Rafe Charnley's son being branded a sheep lover. It don't bear thinking on.'

'That's all that bothers you, isn't it, Pa? Saving your good name and looking tough. It don't bother you none that a man has been killed and you were prepared to do the same to this poor sap.' Jeff helped the sheepman to his feet. He was himself now so incensed that all thought for the consequences of his allegations were ignored. 'Sheepman or cowboy, he's a human being and deserves better than to suffer your wild and reckless actions.'

Charnley spluttered out his own angry riposte. 'How dare you insult me in front of my own men. I ought to — '

'Don't say any more, Pa. You're a big man with a small mind. I don't want anything more to do with you.' He walked over to his horse. 'I'm leaving now. And I won't be back.'

'You durned fool,' Charnley shouted. 'You can't pull out now. I'm ordering you to . . .'

The toothless threat trailed away as

31

the dire import of this awful situation struck home. He struggled to shake off the demons that had addled his thinking. Now bitterly regretting the outburst that had driven a wedge between him and his only son, he tried to retrieve the situation.

'Wait, Jeff, surely we can . . .'

But it was too late. The situation had passed the point of no return. Too many harsh words had been uttered; too much bad blood shed to undo the damage caused to their already strained relationship. There was no going back now.

'Nothing will change my mind now.' Jeff cut his father short while he helped the sheepherder on to a spare horse. 'You'll never change. But this won't be the last you hear of me,' he added in a low voice. 'That I can promise you.'

What he meant by that final prophetic utterance was lost on the distraught rancher. In the space of a few minutes all he had built up was crumbling around him. His head hung low as he watched the two riders depart. Yet still he thought that a stiff response would make things right. He raised an angry fist.

'You'll regret this . . . '

'Let him go, Rafe,' Curly Bob interposed, slinging an arm around his old friend's shoulders. 'The boy will be back once he's simmered down. You just wait and see,' the foreman commiserated, trying to instil some hope of a settlement into the dire situation. A grim cast to his lined features, however, showed that he knew such an outcome was highly unlikely, at least in the near future.

Rigid obstinacy from both parties could not be undone in a hurry. A blatant refusal by both men to cut any slack was going to be their downfall.

Jeff's whole being was trembling with indignation as he rode away, perhaps for ever. Had he burned his boats? Should he have tried to see things from his father's angle? Then the red mist of mule-headedness reasserted itself. His head rose in defiance.

'Much obliged to you, mister, for helping me out back there.' The boy held out a hand, which Jeff shook automatically. 'Figured I was a goner for sure. And I would have been if'n you hadn't stepped in.' Then his young face creased in a look of puzzlement. 'But what made you, a cowman, come to the aid of some jasper you all despise? It don't make no sense to me.'

Jeff's features hardened. 'Not all of us are as stubborn as my father. He can't see beyond his own ambitions. Cattle ranching is everything to him. There's no room for anything else. I reckon that both factions could live amicably if'n they had the will. There's plenty of land for everybody. Some day it will happen.' A listless shrug of the shoulders indicated that he had no great expectation that such a situation would ever occur in his lifetime. 'But my fear is that there's gonna be a lot of needless pain and blood spilt before that.'

The boy nodded in agreement. 'My

pa is of the same mind. Won't budge an inch. We'll all be run off and our flocks destroyed if'n something ain't done soon. And that will cause a range war that nothing can stop.'

Both young men fell into gloomy reflection on the implications of the grim prophecies swirling around inside their heads. Only the gentle rhythmic clipping of shod hoofbeats disturbed the tense silence. The rolling grassland flanking the Big Horn River was interspersed with stands of cotton-woods and dwarf willow. It afforded an ideal terrain for animal farming to flourish. Numerous herds of cattle grazed contentedly on the lush pasture.

But of sheep there was no sign. In the American West of the 1880s, those days were in the distant future.

The young sheepherder broke in on their reverie.

'My name is Sven Fallenborg,' he announced some time later. 'My folks have a small place over the far side of those foothills yonder.'

Jeff looked up. His face displayed shock. 'You ain't gotten a sister called Elsa by any chance, have you?'

This time it was Sven's turn to express surprise. 'You know her?'

The cattleman hesitated. How much should he reveal to this young man? He shrugged. Might as well tell him the whole thing. They were clearly headed in the same direction.

Once he had been apprised of the illicit liaison, Sven assured his saviour that there were no objections where he was concerned, although he expressed doubts as to the future of such a union:

'But my pa won't be so accommodating. You can be sure of that.'

'I ain't planning to whisk her away, if'n that's what he'd be afeared of. Just want to say my goodbyes. There's no knowing when I'll see her again. But one thing is for darned sure though . . .'

Sven's eyebrows lifted as he waited for his companion to continue.

' . . . wherever I decide to settle down, and whatever I choose to do, I want her by my side.'

An hour later, the two riders crossed the western boundary claimed by Rafe Charnley to mark Flying Arrow land. A notice headed by a skull and crossbones depicted the drawing of sheep with a black cross through it. The warning that all such trespassers would be summarily dealt with was unambiguous. It was signed by Rafe Charnley, President of the Big Horn Cattlemen's Association.

Jeff ripped it down. 'This is what a proud nation has come down to. I want no part of it any more.'

Below in a shallow draw lay the blood-stained corpses of half a dozen sheep. Already the scavengers were gathering. A pack of coyotes were picking at the remains. Here was an unexpected but welcome feast. The arrival of the two riders drove them off, temporarily.

'Those were the ones that had strayed on to your land by mistake.' Sven's voice cracked under the emotion of returning to the brutal scene. His eyes welled up. 'It ain't fair. We've done nothing to deserve this sort of treatment.'

Jeff sympathized, but there was nothing he could do now to change things. All he could offer were hollow platitudes.

'At least you are still in one piece. And I'm gonna do my darndest to end this stupid friction between our two camps.'

But for the time being he was helpless.

No further words were necessary from either man as they crested a low knoll up ahead. On the far side in a sheltered glade was the sheep farm run by Joachim Fallenborg. They drew rein overlooking the deceptively tranquil scene. Sheep mooched about chewing on the succulent grass. A woman came out of the cabin to get some water from a well.

Jeff swallowed, his heart skipped a beat. It was Elsa. Sven instructed his companion to wait there while he continued down to the homestead.

'I'll deliver your message,' he murmured somewhat dejectedly. 'Then it's between the two of you what happens next. I guess you'll be pulling out straight away.' Jeff gave a reluctant nod.

A half-smile played across the sheep-herder's dirt-smeared countenance. 'Thanks again for helping me out back there. Reckon I'd have been buzzard bait if'n you hadn't stepped in. I ain't about to forget that.'

Then he spurred the borrowed horse down the slope.

Jeff watched from behind a fallen tree trunk as Sven Fallenborg informed his sister of the recent fracas. The girl looked up towards the knoll but gave no sign that might have been spotted by her judgemental father. The half-hour he was forced to wait on the hill seemed like a lifetime of plagues to the waiting lovelorn Jeff.

He had no option but to cool his heels. Elsa would need to ensure that her temporary departure from the farm was unobserved.

When at last she arrived, the meeting was heartrending for them both. Jeff quickly explained how he had come to find himself in such an intractable situation. Much as she implored him to stay and work things out, the young rancher was adamant that there could be no going back in the current circumstances.

Self-respect and stiff pride demanded the break from family ties, at least for the time being. Etched into his grim features was a hint of the stoic inflexibility so prevalent in the Western male, which precluded any climb-down on his part.

The young man declared a fervent assurance that, as soon as circumstances permitted, he would send word for her to join him. Always assuming that she was still of a mind to become the future Mrs Charnley.

Tears formed in her eyes. She held him tight. How could he doubt her resolve to stay true to the man she loved? Much as he tried to maintain a proudly dispassionate front, the young man could not prevent his own vision misting over. Neither of them wanted the moment to end. But end it must. Jeff gently forced himself to disentangle from his sweetheart's clinging embrace.

Elsa removed a locket from around her neck. Inside was a lock of her blonde hair.

'This will help you remember me through the long dark nights ahead,' she murmured in a tone charged with wistful yearning. 'I will always be here for you, Jeff Charnley. Awaiting the call.' She clutched his hand. 'Just don't make it too long.'

Jeff's throat was dry as the desert wind. Too overcome by emotion, he was lost for words. A mere nod said it all as he mounted up. One final lingering caress, then he forced himself to spur off, only looking back as he reached the crest of the next hill.

The last he saw of Elsa Fallenborg was her wan face framed in a billowing cloud of yellow tresses. Then he was gone.

3

The Man From Wyoming

Jeff Charnley crossed the border into New Mexico two weeks later. The first town he came across was Chama.

He passed the railroad depot, which took up most of the western side. This was where the Cumbres-Toltec line terminated. The railroad provided a vital link into southern Colorado. There was a hint of an extension south to link up with the South Pacific at Albuquerque, but thus far it was only talk. Adjoining the station terminus was a livery stable and the Overland Stagecoach depot. Commercial buildings stretched in a straight line opposite. Two main intersections provided access to housing and various back lots.

Nudging his horse down the main street, Jeff was taken aback by the hive of bustling activity. Flags, bunting and posters welcoming one and all to the town were being erected. Must be some important event, he mused.

He stopped a man who was crossing his path. The bald-headed portly guy was toting a heap of red, white and blue streamers.

'Hold up there, buddy, what goes on here?' he asked. The man looked at this newcomer as if he were from another another planet.

'Gee whiz, mister, where you been?' he exclaimed, almost dropping his goods. 'The annual northern rodeo is due to commence here next week. The place will be buzzing louder than a nest of hornets come Monday week. Everybody round here knows that. Guess you can't be from around these parts.'

'I'm from Wyoming,' Jeff replied. 'We had our rodeo a month ago.'

'You aiming to stick around and try your hand in the ring down here?'

'Could be. Ain't given it any thought until now.'

'Well, best of luck,' remarked the bubbly man. 'But you'll need to be good, with Amos Crowther's Feather Bend crew in the reckoning. Nobody else round here can hold a candle to those punchers.'

At that moment a shout from across the street interrupted the man's flow.

'Get those streamers over here pronto, Chet,' came the lusty summons. 'We still have a heap of work to complete before chow call.'

'Just helping out this stranger,' Chet Stirling called back. 'I'll be right over, boss.' Then he turned back to the newcomer. 'Reckon I'd better be off,' he muttered. 'Dapper Dan don't like to be kept waiting. If'n you do decide to stick around, come over to the Alkali saloon. I'm chief bartender. First drink will be on the house.'

'Much obliged, Chet. I appreciate that,' Jeff thanked the friendly dude, who proceeded across the street at the run.

So he'd arrived just at rodeo time.

Jeff had thought it best to keep quiet about the fact that Wyoming was the home of the first real rodeo on American soil. The Flying Arrow had always taken part and done well.

A sad yearning gripped his innards. His hand strayed to the locket containing the reminder of his sweetheart The lump in his throat made the young rebel question whether he had done the right thing in abandoning his old life. There had been good times when life wasn't so complicated. Now it had all fallen apart.

He quickly threw off the dark mood of doubt. No sense crying over spilt milk. What was done was done. A fresh start beckoned. Chama could be the place to make it happen.

As he pushed on down the bustling thoroughfare he could see, between the buildings, where the pens and compound were being erected on the far side of the town. Rodeos were always the highpoint of a cowboy's year. They offered a good ranch hand the chance to make his mark.

The name rodeo stems from the Spanish for roundup.

Unlike the American affairs, the original Mexican rodeos were more like fiestas, which centred on horse-racing and roping. The Western cowboys north of the border soon adopted the competition. Numerous other activities were added, including, bulldogging, bronc-riding, and bull-wrestling as well as shooting and calf-roping.

They were always well attended, with competitors coming from far and wide to display their skills. Cash prizes way beyond the modest pay of a regular cow-puncher could be won in performing the whole range of ranch-based tasks. It was the silver trophies that were most sought after. A man who carried away a cup could expect to be promoted and would be the envy of his associates.

In the middle of Chama the local sheriff was watching the comings and goings with interest. Heck Toomey was talking to another man. They were naturally discussing the imminent event that would attract all kinds of folk.

It was a time when a lawman needed to be especially alert. As well as honest, hard-working competitors, there would be the inevitable riff-raff hoping to con the gullible punters out of their winnings.

His companion was Amos Crowther. The two men were good friends.

'You aiming to clear up again this year, Amos?' The lawman's inquiry intimated that he fully expected his buddy to win most of the competitions. 'You didn't give the others much of a chance last year.'

The Feather Bend was the biggest cattle ranch at the north end of the Arriba Valley. Crowther always excused his top hands from their regular jobs at rodeo time to ensure they were well practised in all the contests. It was a matter of pride and prestige. The rancher naturally enjoyed the kudos that winning brought.

But it was also financially lucrative. His men might win the trophies and dough, but success brought the name of the Feather Bend to the attention of important buyers in the East. That was worth far more to Crowther than anything else. He could ask a higher price for his beef as a result, and there would be no quibbling and haggling.

'I ain't one to blow my own trumpet, Heck,' said the rancher disingenuously, hooking his thumbs into a silk vest, 'but there sure ain't nobody around here that can touch my boys when it comes to rodeoing.'

'You never know,' replied the sheriff, hoping to dent his friend's pompous assertion. 'You might be surprised this year. I hear tell there's jaspers coming in from Texas to compete. It shows what a big event this has become. You confident enough to handle guys like that?'

Crowther poured scorn on the insinuation. 'They'll have to be darned good to best my hands. Reckon those cups will be occupying pride of place in my trophy room once again, Heck.' He pulled out a couple of best Havana cigars and handed one to the sheriff. They lit up before Crowther puffed out his chest adding, 'Yessirree, the Feather Bend will take some beating.'

Heck Toomey smothered a grin as his friend twisted the ends of his thick black moustache.

'How's about we mosey on down to the Alkali and I'll buy you a drink to celebrate my impending victory?' the rancher suggested.

'A mite premature, ain't you, old buddy?'

Crowther shrugged. 'In the bag, Heck, in the bag. Anyway, enough about that. Estelle has been asking when you're coming over for dinner again. She ain't seen you for a couple of weeks. When you gonna propose to her? You two have been walking out for some time now. Can't have my best gal left sitting on the fence.'

Much to his old buddy's delight, Rio Arriba's tough sheriff could not suppress a blushing countenance. He had been courting the comely sister of his friend for three months. Their relationship had so far been somewhat restrained. A few tentative kisses on the cheek were as far as any romantic association had progressed, due to the shy attitude of both parties. Heck did not say anything, but he was hoping to plight his troth more positively during rodeo week.

Crowther appeared to read his thoughts. A deep grin spread across his weathered face as he repeated his light-hearted quip. 'So when are you gonna make an honest woman of my sister, Heck?'

The sheriff blushed even more. Muttering some trifling asides, he brushed off the query. He had no wish to discuss his burgeoning relationship with anyone at the moment. Instead he quickly changed the subject as they continued along the boardwalk.

'Did you hear about old Dekon Janus selling up? He told me he's getting too old for this game and is heading for California.'

Effectively sidetracked by the topic of cattle business, Crowther nodded. 'His spread is up for sale. There's gonna be an auction this afternoon.'

'It backs on to your place, don't it?'

'Sure does. I bought his stock. That Angus bull and his Durham shorthorns are just what I need to improve my own breeds. I gave him a good price too. Now let's go get us that drink.'

'Ain't you making a bid for the land?' Toomey inquired.

Crowther gave a vigorous shake of his head. 'No chance. Most of it is grazed out. Maybe that's why he's leaving. Only thing fit for that scrub now is sheep.'

It was a throwaway remark that was to have devastating consequences.

The two men were about to continue across the street when they were interrupted by a rider who was just passing.

'Pardon me for butting in, gents,' the man apologized, tipping his hat. 'But I couldn't help overhearing you say there was a spread for sale in this area. I'd sure be interested if'n the price is right.'

Sheriff Toomey appraised the tall rider. He was a stranger. The guy's clothes were of good quality if a tad on the dusty side, a fact that told the lawman he had clearly been on the trail for some time.

'And who might you be, mister?' The query was delivered in a friendly if direct manner.

'Jeff Charnley from up Wyoming way,' the man replied.

'I thought you must have been on the trail for some time. That horse you're riding is a mighty fine-looking animal.'

Jeff tweaked Buster's ears. The blue roan snickered and shook his head. 'I bought him from a Nez Percé breeder up in Montana. Those Indians special-ize in these horses. I'd challenge anyone to find a better mount anywhere.'

Crowther's condescending regard indi-cated that he was not impressed. Loftily he replied, 'Maybe if you plan to stick around, you could enter him in the race next week at the rodeo.' A leery smirk creased the rancher's face. 'Although I wouldn't give you much hope against my palomino. Nothing on four legs has ever beaten Flash. What do you reckon, Heck?'

'Ain't my call, Amos. You're the guy who figures he has everyone beat.'

The two men held each other's gaze. Without altering his deadpan expression, Jeff replied softly, 'There's always a first time, mister. Maybe this is it.' Without waiting for the rancher to respond to the slight, Jeff addressed the sheriff. 'Perhaps you could point me in the direction of the land agent charged with the sale?'

'The agent's name is Sam Hogan and his office is up the street on the left. He'll give you all the information you need. Good luck, young fella.'

'Obliged to you, Sheriff.' Then to Amos Crowther, he added, 'Make sure your cayuse is on top form, mister, if'n you plan on running him agin Buster here. Cos he'll need to be.' Then he spurred off.

'Seems like that guy has found your

measure, Amos,' Toomey chuckled.

'Cocky young whippersnapper!' The rancher bristled. 'Thinks he can outrun Flash, does he? Ugh! Ain't gotten a hope in Hades.'

The lawman couldn't help noticing that his friend was somewhat shaken by the challenge. When Amos Crowther stroked his chin, it meant something had spooked him. And that, clearly, was the man from Wyoming.

The next day Jeff Charnley was passing the sheriff's office.

'How did you get on with Hogan, Mr Charnley?' Toomey called out.

The young man's face was wreathed in smiles. He swung Buster over to join the lawman outside his office.

'Mr Hogan took me out there and showed me around. The place is perfect for what I want. It has water and a ready-made cabin and barn, all in good condition. There were some other guys interested. But I offered him the fixed price with no quibbling and he was glad to accept it. All I need to do now is arrange a bank transfer from my account in Casper, Wyoming.'

Heck Toomey was drawn into the young guy's eagerness and impressed by his diligent organization. There was a spirit of enterprise there that was sadly lacking in many young cowpokes. He could see this guy going places.

So why had he come all this way south from Wyoming? Surely there were equally good spreads up there. The investigative streak in all good officers hinted that it might be worth looking into at some point. Perhaps, when the rodeo had finished, he would make some discreet inquiries.

'Wish me luck, Sheriff.'

'Seems to me that you don't need any luck,' the lawman declared. 'You sure ain't one to let the grass grow under your feet.'

'Strike while the iron is hot, that's my motto, Sheriff,' replied the newcomer briskly. 'Not only that, I've ordered in fresh stock and hired me some hands to help drive them down there. The animals will be arriving here on the first train day after tomorrow.'

'Have you moved in there yet?'

'My next call is to hire a wagon and buy in some supplies. Reckon I'll be settled in by tonight.'

'Good luck anyway.' Toomey was genuine in his wish for the capable young rancher to make a success of his new enterprise. 'I'll be down at the depot to watch the proceedings.'

4

Unwelcome Arrivals

A couple of days later a lonesome-sounding whistle heralded the arrival of the early-morning train. The first two cars were for passengers. The attention of one man on the platform was focused on the last two. While the conductor made the announcement that Chama was the end of the line, Jeff Charnley made his way to the end freight cars. Following behind him were three men hired to drive the animals back to his newly purchased holding.

'Glad to see the train's on time,' Sheriff Toomey remarked to the conductor. 'Last week I was stuck here waiting five hours.'

'That was because of a landslide in Conejos Canyon,' replied the aggrieved official. 'It was cleared the same day and the loose banking shored up. It won't happen again, Sheriff. Of that I can assure you. The company is most proud to maintain its reputation for good timekeeping.'

'Glad to hear it,' snorted Toomey. 'I don't want dangerous prisoners hanging around a station platform. They could decide to make a run for freedom.'

With a sniffy twitch of his moustache, the conductor turned on his heel. He called to the new rancher.

'Your stock is in freight car number two, Mr Charnley. Be quick and unload it if'n you please; we have to be ready for the return journey in a half-hour.' He peered down at his pocket watch to emphasize the need for urgency.

'OK, boys, we'll drive them over to the stock pens until I've sorted out the paperwork,' Jeff ordered his men. He led them over to the rear car. 'Vegas, you open the door while Jingle Zeb and Laredo get ready to keep 'em from straying.'

Vegas Crabbe heaved on the door lever and forced it down to release the heavy sliding door. Peering inside the car, the burly cowhand received the shock of his life.

'What in thunder is going on here!' he exclaimed, stepping back.

The others moved forward to see what had spooked their buddy. A dirty white sea of wool greeted their ogling peepers.

Sheep! The detested bleating assaulted their ears as the animals struggled to escape from the confines of their prison.

'Damn blasted, sheep,' growled Zeb Tankred, angrily stamping his boots on the wooden platform. The jingle bobs affixed to his spurs chattered out their own unmusical chorus. 'What game you playing, Charnley? We didn't sign on to herd these scummy beasts.' Laredo pushed the young herdsman, who fell over one of the skittish animals. 'This is cattle country. You can't run sheep here.'

The three men hovered over their fallen employer. Angry scowls and bunched fists augured trouble with a big 'T'.

'We quit, Charnley,' Crabbe snarled, voicing what all three of the newly hired hands were thinking. 'You tricked us. We naturally figured you were bringing in steers.' A boot was launched at the fallen man. Jeff couldn't avoid the vicious blow which sent a barb of pain down his leg. 'Even the extra pay you promised won't persuade me to herd sheep,' the angry puncher growled. 'Come on, boys,' he called to his sidekicks. 'Let's go get a drink to wash the stink of these critters from our throats.'

'That guy's a crazy loon if'n he thinks he can bring sheep on to this range,' Tankred cursed over his shoulder at the startled sheepman, who was struggling to his feet.

Grumbling and muttering, the three men strutted off.

With nobody to keep them under control, the sheep tumbled out of the car. In the time it takes to say woolly jumper, they were hollering and bleating. Released from custody they milled about the train depot.

'Get those animals off the rail line,' shouted the conductor, waving his arms as he hurried over. 'Ain't you got no sense, mister?'

Sheriff Toomey had been reading the latest edition of the New Mexico Herald when the fracas began. Looking up, all he could see was a sea of white rolling across the street, threatening to run wild. Tossing the paper aside he called to the blundering figure of Jeff Charnley.

'Hey there, fella! Stop them right away or those critters will be all over the town.'

Removing his hat and waving his outstretched arms, the lawman dashed into the street. 'Come on, yuh durned fool,' he admonished the startled sheepman. 'This ain't no time for dithering about. Help me get these brutes into the pens.'

Quickly recovering his wits, Jeff

joined the sheriff.

'Scat, you blasted varmints,' he railed angrily. 'Heeeyaaaah!'

Dust and the hated stink of sheep pervaded the whole of the north end of the town. Luckily sheep are much easier to herd than cattle and the two men soon managed to head them off. A dog suddenly decided to join in the fun. Yapping and snapping at their heels, the unwitting creature added some much needed extra help.

The sheep were herded back in the direction of the pens, where they were soon corralled, but it had been touch and go. Toomey slammed the gate shut.

'By glory, that was close,' he gasped out, drawing much-needed air into his lungs. The sheriff beat vigorously at his clothes to disperse the dust. Sharp barbs of exasperation pricked his sun-ripened features. Purposefully he stormed across to the sheepherder.

'What in thunderation are you doing, Charnley?' The sheriff was well aware of the fury that the arrival of the sheep would arouse. The last thing he needed was a range war. 'This is only the beginning of your troubles if'n you keep hold of these critters. Cattlemen don't take kindly to having sheep on their land. There's gonna be big trouble if'n you carry on like this.'

'Far as I am aware, Sheriff, this is open country.' Jeff was not about to back down to any browbeating from anybody. He held his temper with some effort before delivering a measured but decisive response. 'Nobody is going to drive me off'n the land I have bought and paid for. There ain't no law says I can't run sheep. So that's what I aim to do. I just want to be left alone to run my own affairs. Is that so wrong?'

'It is where sheep are involved,' Toomey insisted, trying to make the young man see sense. 'This is gonna create bad feeling all round. Why don't you just forget about it? Best thing for you to do is sell up and head back to Wyoming.'

Jeff was not listening. The last thing

he intended was returning home with his tail between his legs. He could imagine his father's reaction if that was to happen.

'This is my home now, and I intend making a go of it,' Jeff replied firmly. 'I thank you for helping me corral these animals. Now I'd be obliged if'n you would allow me to get about the business of herding them down to my spread. Any ideas where I can hire some hands who ain't prejudiced against sheep?'

Heck Toomey knew there was no point in pressing his case. This guy was stubborn and ornery. He had dug in his heels. All he could hope was that the ranchers would leave the guy alone. His job was to keep the peace.

'The only fools who are likely to accept your offer are stumblebums and layabouts,' the sheriff declared. 'No regular hand will give you the time of day once they all learn what you're trying to do.'

With that blunt declaration he turned

on his heel, mumbling to himself about all the unwanted problems this ornery knucklehead had landed him with.

Jeff stood in the middle of the street, hands on hips, wondering how he was going to get his new acquisitions back to the ranch. The outburst at the rail depot had attracted a host of onlookers. Hostile eyes stabbed at the young sheepherder who had dug his heels in. Looks of stony indifference were thrown at him as he made his way over to the pens.

But there was one present who was ready and willing to lend a hand. He nuzzled the man's leg, a low whine drawing Jeff's attention down to the helpful mutt who had stepped in at the crucial moment.

Jeff's face lit up. 'Well, by hokey!' he exclaimed in jubilant surprise. 'Guess I ain't alone after all.' He stroked the scrawny animal's head, receiving a bark of bright-eyed joy in reply. 'You want to sign on then, fella?' he inquired, a broad grin easing away the worry lines creasing his tanned features. 'Reckon you've earned your pay helping me out just now. We'll soon have you fed and watered once the sheep are settled on our spread. You all set for some more work?'

The dog jumped about, eager to display his innate talent.

'Then let's go.'

Sheriff Toomey shook his head as he watched the sheepman disappear into the pen. 'Trouble, trouble and more trouble. That's what you spell, mister,' he muttered under his breath. But where was it going to come from first? That was the main question. For come it surely would. No doubt about it. And Heck Toomey would be stuck in the middle, as ever, trying to keep the peace.

The hassle he was expecting came four days later.

Heck was checking the recently erected corrals and the safety of the two audience stands at the rodeo site. He had buried the problem of Jeff Charnley at the back of his mind and had almost forgotten about it when a dust-stained rider thundered across the open ground. Dragging the lathered bay to a stumbling halt, he leapt out of the saddle and hurried across.

'What's gotten you in such a sweat, Milldew?' the sheriff asked, pausing in his task.

Milldew Haywain was the wrangler for the Broken Wheel ranch at the bottom end of the valley.

'I was passing close to that new guy's spread over on Saltpan Flats when Amos Crowther and his boys passed me. When I inquired where they were headed, Amos said they were gonna fix the sheepman proper. Did I want to go along and enjoy the fun?'

Toomey's eyes widened. He had expected something to blow up. But he hadn't reckoned on his old buddy being behind it.

'Guess you must have turned him down.' It was a statement of fact. Haywain's appearance here proved that.

'I ain't no fan of sheep. None of us

are. But violence like what Crowther is planning ain't the answer.'

'Much obliged for your warning, Milldew,' the sheriff replied, cursing under his breath. 'I'd best get over there pronto and put a stop to this fracas.'

Leaving the rodeo arena, Toomey rode back into Chama to collect his rifle and gunbelt. He could only pray that he would be in time to prevent any rash action by his reckless friend. Amos had expressed his anger in no uncertain terms at the arrival of sheep on the range, but Toomey had not expected an outburst of indignation like this, at least not until after the rodeo had finished. Clearly he had underestimated Crowthor's burning hatred of all things woolly.

Urging his horse to the gallop, the sheriff cut across country. It was rougher than the regular trail, but with care it should save him a good hour; every minute was going to be vital if he was to maintain the peace.

* ★ ★

Amos Crowther and his men were gathered together on a low hill overlooking the cabin now occupied by the detested sheep-pusher. They had been careful to tether their mounts well out of sight. The sheep could be seen nibbling away at the pasture beyond the far side of the cabin. They were edging ever nearer to the boundary of Crowther's land. The rancher scowled. Too darned close for comfort.

He was determined not to allow these trespassers to settle in the Arriba Valley. Allow one outfit to make a success of it and others would surely follow. In a blink of an eye they would be swamped with the vile creatures. No! It had to be nipped in the bud. And he was the guy to do it.

'This is it, boys,' he whispered. 'We'll spread out and surround the place. That jasper can't be allowed to escape.' He held his men's gaze in a steely glare. 'Understand me?'

Brisk nods followed. These men were no less biased against the woolly invasion than their boss.

'Keep your guns handy. But don't make a move until after I've given him the ultimatum. If'n the jackass proves awkward, he'll soon find what happens when sheep are brought into cattle country.'

'Do we torch the place, boss?' asked a grinning Vegas Crabbe.

He and his two sidekicks had hurried back to the Feather Bend once they had discovered the truth about their new boss. Excuses had been manufactured on the way to explain their sudden departure.

Crowther had railed and grumbled, threatening to throw the three slimeballs off his spread, but he needed them for what he had in mind. Crabbe and his buddies might not be top cowhands, but they were handy with their guns. That was what counted now. The most important issue was to prevent sheep taking over on land where cattle had priority.

'Only if'n he refuses to walk away,' replied Crowther, checking his hardware. 'We have to do this according to the law. Give the sap the chance to see the error of his ways. No one can say that Amos Crowther ain't a law-abiding citizen.' He smirked at the hovering men. 'Just so long as the guy does as he's told.' Guffaws all round gave the small gathering a dark aura of menace. 'OK, boys, let's go clear up this sheep dung.'

Crowther allowed his men time to get into position before making his presence known.

'Hey, you in the cabin,' he called out gruffly. 'This is Amos Crowther of the Feather Bend. You're trespassing, mister. This is cattle country and sheep ain't welcome in the Arriba. Leave now without any fuss and I'll make sure you don't lose out on the sale.' He paused to give the galoot time to consider the proposition. 'It's a generous offer. So how about you coming outside so we can talk it through man to man?'

For a moment there was no reply. Then a puff of smoke wafted from one of the windows in the cabin. It was followed a throaty roar as a bullet lifted the hat from Crowther's head.

'Aaaagh!' The startled ranch boss howled in shock, then dropped to the ground.

'That's your answer, Crowther,' came the angry retort from the cabin's occupant. 'And there'll be more of the same if'n you try to force me out.' To lend emphasis to his rebuttal of Crowther's intimidating threat, another bullet ploughed a furrow close to the cattleman's boot heel. 'You got the message now?'

Charnley's new sheepherder added a strident accompaniment of angry barking to his boss's stubborn refusal to be browbeaten into surrender.

To save face in front of his men, Crowther replied with his own bullyboy rejoinder. He levered a round into the chamber of his Winchester carbine.

'All right, Charnley, you've had your

chance. Now face the consequences. Let him have it, boys!'

A fusillade of shots rang out as a dozen guns let rip.

But before the battle could proceed to its gruesome climax a full-throated shout from behind stayed the trigger fingers of the ambushers.

'Hold on there! Put up your guns. First man who fires another shot will find himself stoking in hell.'

'What the heck . . . ?' exclaimed Vegas Crabbe.

'It's the sheriff,' gasped Laredo Fudge in a worried bleat.

Both of his six shooters palmed, Heck Toomey leapt off his horse. Even though he was only one man, Toomey had a reputation that only the most rash of gunslingers would challenge. All those present knew about the sheriff's past achievements in the field of law enforcement.

Before arriving in Chama he had single-handedly cleaned up Durango, over the border in Colorado. Before that it had been Dodge City, where his guns had remained firmly in their holsters. Meaty fists like hammers had effectively subdued those who chose to buck the system.

Only once had Toomey needed to respond with gunfire.

Tramp Thewlis, a local tough, had heard the sheriff's crunching denunciation of his attempt to gain a free meal from Chang Hai's Cantonese Diner. He'd run off down an alley before an arrest could be made.

Later the same day the somewhat inebriated braggart called Toomey out for a middle-of-the-street showdown. The two-gun lawman had tried unsuccessfully to defuse the situation. But Thewlis was adamant that he had been served up slop that a dog wouldn't touch. It was the chiselling Chinaman who ought to be arrested.

'Funny that you managed to shovel it all down,' Toomey remarked. 'Not the behaviour of a man claiming to have been poisoned.'

Thewlis had no answer to that except to go for his gun. Two bullets, one from each of the marshal's Colt Frontier six-shooters, drilled the challenger squarely in the chest.

The job of county sheriff for Rio Arriba had been offered to Toomey soon after. It was a step up the ladder. A rise in pay plus accommodation found the tough lawman crossing the border into New Mexico. That had been a year before.

'Looks like I arrived just in time,' he snapped. 'What you playing at, Amos? I figured you would know better than to take the law into your own hands. There'll be no vigilante settlement of disputes in my jurisdiction. Any problems you have, I'll be the one to sort them out.'

'I ain't got no quarrel with you, Heck,' Crowther replied, holstering his revolver, 'but this legal stuff can take for ever. We need action fast. You know what sheepmen are like. They put up fencing, and those darned beasts destroy the pasture with their sharp hoofs. I could name a whole heap of guys in this valley who'd back my play. You should be supporting those that voted you into office, not siding with this dirty scumbag.'

'Bullets aren't the way to solve disputes,' replied Toomey, standing his ground. His guns were still aimed at the scowling Feather Bend riders. 'You should have talked to him first.'

'Didn't I try all that, boys?' Crowther appealed to his men. 'But he didn't want to know.'

'It was Charnley that started the shooting, Sheriff,' Jingle Zeb Tankred piped up. 'You can't expect us to sit back when the guy's out to gun us down.' His two buddies nodded vigorously in agreement. They were still smarting from Charnley's trickery in leading them to believe he was a cattleman.

'What would you do when a pile of jaspers start throwing their weight around?' Toomey's usual tolerant manner was becoming overheated and more than a tad exasperated by the bickering. 'I'm telling you again. There'll be no gun law in this county. What the hell! Are you out to start a range war?' He jabbed an accusing finger at the rancher. 'If'n anything happens to Charnley, I'll see you brought before the courts for murder.'

Crowther's face clouded over. 'I thought you were my friend. You shouldn't be going down on the side of a sheepshank. It ain't right.'

Toomey moved close to his old buddy. His face was devoid of expression. But the diamond hard glint in his eyes portended dire consequences. The noses of the two men were almost touching as the lawman delivered his pronouncement.

'Some things are above friendship. Nobody and nothing is above the law. You go against that and I'll see you hang. Now get your horses and go back to doing the business you know.'

Nothing more was said as the surly rancher led his muttering crew away.

A mark had been overstepped. Nothing could ever be the same between the two old friends now. But where sheep were involved, Amos Crowther refused to see reason. It was him or them.

For the time being, however, he would have to curb his impatience and wait for the right moment to come.

5

No Damned Water

For the next few days nothing untoward was reported. Heck Toomey was arriving at the welcome conclusion that his old pal had decided to try cooperating for once.

Preparations for the forthcoming rodeo were keeping everyone busy. Crowther would be anxious to retain the championship trophy he had won the previous year. Toomey was sure that the Feather Bend would be putting in a great deal of practice to hone their skills to perfection in all the events.

More competitors were arriving every day from all over the territory and beyond. It was all set to be the best show ever, and the town would benefit greatly from the extra business.

The sheriff hooked his boots on to

the scarred desk and leaned back in his rocking-chair. It was late afternoon. Deputy Hemp Drucker would be taking over the evening shift soon. Toomey stretched the tiredness from his muscles. It had been a busy few days. He tipped his hat and settled comfortably into his chair. His peepers flickered drowsily and closed. In the beat of a gnat's wing he was fast asleep. The gentle murmur of snoring filled the office.

It seemed no more than a few seconds since Toomey had succumbed to the lure of Orpheus when a furious hammering on the outside door broke into his addled brain. He struggled to wakefulness as the thumping was repeated.

'You in there, Sheriff?' came the brusque demand from outside.

Without waiting for a reply, two men barged into the office.

'What in tarnation!' Toomey grumbled. 'Who told you to barge in — ?'

The spokesman cut short the disgruntled protest. 'Somebody is tampering with the valley water supply, Sheriff,' snorted

Ezra Carp, a small-time rancher with a big voice, which he was exercising now to its full capacity. Anger bubbled on Carp's ruddy face as he shook his fist. 'The creek is so low you can walk across without getting your feet wet.'

'That dam up in the Questa mountains is supposed to have regulated the flow,' added the other rancher. Jubal Stokes ran the Broken Wheel and was inclined to put their case in a much calmer and more reasoned delivery. Yet even he was showing signs of exasperation. 'Every outfit in the valley is affected and they've sent us along to see what you aim to do about it.'

Toomey was well aware that Amos Crowther had built the dam high up in the mountains after experiencing the fickle nature of the rainfall. The sudden storms that rapidly built up over the rugged terrain had deluged the valley, causing floods. At other times in the hot dry summers, drought had so parched the ground as to leave it cracked and devoid of growth for the cattle.

One season of the unpredictable weather was enough for the new rancher. He had used his own funds to finance the venture which now effectively controlled the water supply for the whole valley. In periods of heavy rainfall the sluice was closed and the water allowed to back up behind the dam. In contrast, a regulated flow during the dry period gave everybody an even supply of the precious commodity.

A yearly charge was made for this vital service, which all the ranchers were more than happy to pay. It had worked efficiently for twenty years. This was the first instance of a breakdown in the system.

The sheriff rubbed his stubble-coated chin. His firm brow furrowed in thought. 'Mighty strange,' he murmured. 'Mighty strange.'

'We're paying Amos Crowther for a regular water supply,' snapped Carp, who was less than enthused by the lawman's laconic manner. 'This problem is his responsibility and needs sorting out fast.'

Charnley's sheep would need water as much as would the cattle outfits. After their recent fracas Toomey would not put it past the owner of the Feather Bend to pull a devious stunt like this. He needed regulated water just like the others, but the Carrizo Creek, which had its source in the Questas, cut across the north-west corner of Crowther's land. So he could call on a subsidiary supply should the need arise.

Toomey's features hardened. All the signs pointed to his old buddy jeopardizing the other ranchers in pursuit of his blatant vendetta against the sheepman, but until he had solid evidence to support his suspicions he would keep quiet. No sense in throwing out random accusations without proof.

'I'll ride out to the dam and take a look first thing in the morning,' he promised the two men. 'Leave it with me. And rest assured that I'll leave no stone unturned in getting to the bottom of this without delay.'

'Make sure you do,' griped Carp.

His associate quickly ushered the grumpy rancher towards the door. 'We're obliged, Sheriff,' Stokes said. 'Ezra knows you'll clear it up, don't you, buddy?' He dug an elbow into his friend's ribs.

'Ugh!' was the noncommittal reply.

* * *

Even before the first rays of the new day had gleamed through the Questas' serrated rim Heck Toomey was on the trail. A two-hour ride brought him to the foothills of the looming mountain range. A narrow trail snaked up between stands of pine, then led into a broad ravine down which the bubbling waters of the Rio Arriba were meant to flow.

In the normal course of events, at this time of year the cataract would have been in full spate. But today it was little more than a trickle.

Those guys sure weren't exaggerating, Toomey mused. This is serious. A few days with no water in the heat of summer could have disastrous consequences, especially for the small outfits. He climbed higher into the mountain fastness until the dam came into view.

It was an awesome sight. This was the first time that Heck Toomey had been up here. His eyes widened as the full extent of the construction and its resulting containment struck home.

This upper section of the Arriba Valley was a huge amphitheatre high above the main valley. A giant might easily have scooped out the bowl with a ladle and tossed the detritus aside. The resultant configuration offered the perfect facility for storing water. The original tiny lake had now grown into a broad expanse.

The lawman could not help but acknowledge the foresight and good judgement displayed by Amos Crowther. The rancher's decision to control the unpredictable nature of the rainwater was a stroke of genius. For upwards of five minutes Toomey just stared at the large stretch of water.

Ducks and other wildfowl were floating contentedly upon the tranquil surface.

What became immediately obvious was that the reservoir had been allowed to build up to an unprecedented level. The sheriff dismounted and moved across to inspect the sluice gate in the middle of the structure. It was operated by a winding lever which controlled the release or otherwise of the reserve of water behind.

Closer observation revealed the grim truth. The well-oiled mechanism was virtually closed. A small amount of water was being allowed to dribble through the gap as a token offering to prevent the reservoir from overflowing. The idea was clearly to give the impression that no skulduggery had been perpetrated. Toomey was not fooled in the least. This was unlawful duplicity on a grand scale.

Here was all the proof the lawman needed that somebody had deliberately engineered the reduction of the water supply to the lower valley. There could only be one culprit to blame for this heinous action. Toomey was nonplussed. How could such a well-respected rancher and businessman of Amos Crowther's standing resort to such vindictive tactics?

In recent days he had witnessed a new side to the man he had come to regard as a friend. The lawman's face set in a grim resolve. Action was needed to confront the perpetrator with his skulduggery and resolve the matter forthwith.

Just as he was turning away to mount up, the sun reflected off a shiny object close to the edge of the dam. Toomey wandered across and picked up a silver teardrop. They usually came in pairs and were affixed to a rider's spurs. A gleam of triumph lit the lawman's eyes. Find the owner of the missing jingle bob and he had his culprit.

With renewed determination, Toomey mounted up and swung his horse back down the trail. At the bottom of the steep downfall, he veered off to head in the direction of the Feather Bend. The owner had some serious questions to answer.

The sheriff's arrival beneath an entrance archway surmounted by a broad set of longhorns was met with curious glances. More hands than normal were in the vicinity. It was clear that they were all honing their individual skills for participation in the forthcoming rodeo.

The sheriff was normally a welcome visitor to the ranch, but the recent showdown at the sheep farm had left a sour taste in the mouth. The atmosphere was tense as men openly arrowed hostile looks at the starpacker. Loyalties were clearly with the man who paid their wages.

Crowther had noticed his old friend's arrival and now met him on the veranda of the main ranch house. His thumbs were stuck in his belt. Legs apart, he displayed the lofty arrogance of a man confident in his own domain.

'Didn't expect a visit from you in a hurry after our last run-in,' he declared emphatically. 'I ain't too sure if'n you're welcome on Feather Bend land.'

'This is official business, Amos,' the sheriff announced bluntly. 'Mind if'n I step down?'

'Help yourself.' Crowther shrugged. 'So what's this all about? That scummy sheep-dipper been complaining? I ain't been nowhere near his place since you warned me off.'

'I have reason to believe that somebody has been tampering with the water supply up on the Questa Dam. The other ranchers in the valley have complained that the water has been cut off. I've just come from the dam and it's true. The sluice has been virtually closed to shut off the water. This has to be your doing, Amos. I never figured you for a guy who would be prepared to jeopardize the other spreads just to drive Charnley out.'

Crowther was stunned by the accusation. His mouthed flapped like a hooked trout on a line before he managed to articulate a vehement denial.

'That's a load of eyewash. I ain't been up to the dam for more than two weeks. Where's your proof that it was me?'

'Somebody dropped this up there.' The sheriff slowly produced the shiny teardrop. 'Only dude I know around here that wears these baubles is Jingle Zeb Tankred. And he's one of your boys.'

Crowther looked genuinely stunned on being presented with this revelation. Momentarily lost for words, he stared at the damning evidence.

'I don't know anything about this. That's the honest truth, Heck. I would never expose the valley to this kind of danger. I have more to lose than anybody.'

'What about the spare water from Carrizo Creek?' An accusation was clearly implied.

'That's not enough for the number of cattle I run. You know that.' Crowther waved his arms in an attempt to stress his ignorance of the odious offence.

Then the dark lines of anger altered his ruddy features. He immediately called to the nearest man: 'Where's Tankred and his sidekicks?'

'Last I saw they were practising calf-roping round the back of the barn,' replied an old hand called Strongbow Curry.

'Get them over here, pronto,' snapped Crowther.

Recognizing the urgency in the order Strongbow hurried across to the barn.

Toomey couldn't help but smile at the peculiar rolling gait characteristic of a life spent in the saddle. A few minutes later the three men appeared. On spotting the sheriff talking to their boss, Vegas Crabbe eyed his buddies nervously. What was this about? The unspoken fear that something untoward was afoot gripped his innards.

The spokesman of the trio, Crabbe tried to paste a nonchalant expression on to his coarse visage. 'Some'n the matter, boss?'

'You know darned well what's up!'

rasped Crowther, squaring his shoulders. 'This was found up near the Questa Dam.' The rancher held out the silver bauble.

On beholding the single spur adornment, the automatic reaction of Jingle Zeb was to peer down at his left boot heel. He knew the item had gone missing but had no idea where he'd lost it. The movement was a sure sign of guilt.

'It was you three that turned off the sluice up there, wasn't it?' growled the ranch boss. 'I never gave the order to do that. Why in tarnation did you clowns pull a fool stunt like that?'

'We figured to be doing you a favour, boss,' said Laredo Fudge, in an attempt to excuse their nefarious action. The real reason was to assuage their humiliation at being hoodwinked by the sheepherder. 'We figured that having the water cut off would drive that sheep dude off the range.'

'And the rest of the ranchers as well, you fools,' growled the angry cattleman.

'Grab your gear and clear out. You're all fired.'

Now it was Toomey's turn to step forward. The sheriff was aware that he needed to take decisive action in order to satisfy the ranchers who had lodged the complaint. 'Not so fast,' he rapped out. 'This is a serious incident. I'm arresting you three for illegally trying to sabotage the livelihoods of a lot of honest people in the valley.'

For a moment nobody moved. But the sheriff quickly noted a hint of resistance twisting Vegas Crabbe's thin lips.

'Better come quietly, or it'll be the worse for you.'

Crabbe had already sampled the dubious delights of the territorial prison at Santa Fe and had no wish to renew an acquaintance. He backed off, his right hand already dropping to the gun on his hip.

'Nobody is taking me in.'

Within seconds the morning's usual calm was shattered by gunfire.

Crabbe's first shot missed its mark. His second took Crowther in the forearm. The rancher staggered back holding the injured limb.

Toomey drew his own pistol and pumped a couple of shots at the three men. Laredo went down, shot through the chest. Crabbe was still backing away towards the sheriff's horse. Another shot lifted the lawman's hat, causing Toomey to duck down.

Smoke filled the air. The acrid smell of cordite clutched at the men's throats.

Taking advantage of the sudden mêlée, Tankred saw his opportunity to drill the sheriff from the side. His gun rose.

Caught on the hop by the sudden upsurge of violence, the rest of the hands took cover. This was not their fight. Only Strongbow Curry stood his ground even though he was momentarily paralyzed. But his sharp gaze noticed Tankred's sneaky manoeuvre. The boss was in danger. Exhibiting a total disregard for his own safety, the old guy hollered out a warning. He then launched his lean frame at the gunnie. Both men went down in a heap. The gun in Tankred's hand went off.

Curry was in the way of the bullet. He had no chance and was killed instantly. Toomey immediately swung to cover the killer.

'Drop your gun or die, you son of Satan!' he snarled out. The jingle man was past the point of no return. His gun swung towards the sheriff. A single blast from the lawman's pistol finished him off.

Hearing the noise of battle, a woman emerged from the hen house. Estelle Crowther, the rancher owner's sister, had been inside gathering up the day's supply of eggs. She was clutching a basket in her hands when she found herself at the mercy of Vegas Crabbe. An opportunity not to be missed had presented itself. He grabbed a firm hold of the woman, his gun roughly prodding her swanlike neck.

'Come any closer and the woman

gets it,' he snapped. 'I'm leaving and she's coming with me. Try to follow and her blood will be on your hands.'

The blunt warning was for the sheriff, who was cursing his impotence. 'Harm one hair of her head and you're a dead man,' he shouted.

Seeing the woman he loved in such dire straits and being unable to help felt like a knife twisting in his guts. It took all his willpower to restrain an intense desire to rush the guy. But the sheriff knew that Crabbe's threat was no idle bluff. What had been a minor incident with probably a six-month sentence at most had quickly gravitated into a brutal gun fight.

Crabbe knew it. He had acted by instinct. Any regrets were now meaningless.

The hangman's noose was hovering. He punched out a bitter guffaw while dragging the woman over to the horse. There he heaved her across the saddle horn before scrambling up behind.

'I'll be keeping a watch on my back

trail,' he called out. 'Any sign of dust . . . ' He left the threat unspoken. The direful message was unequivocal. 'Once I'm clear, then I'll think about letting her go. But that's up to you. So long, suckers.'

6

Scruff Takes a Hand

Once satisfied that nobody was on his tail Crabbe decided to set the woman adrift. She was slowing him down. He needed to be over the border into Colorado before nightfall. Then he would be home and dry.

During the brief flight from the Feather Bend the heady scent from Estelle Crowther's lustrous hair and body had quickly stimulated the lustful juices churning away in his loins. Vegas Crabbe had always fancied the comely dame. Now was his chance to take advantage of her vulnerable situation.

Another quick glance to the rear revealed no sign of trail dust. Those critters had obviously taken his warning seriously. Up ahead was a shallow draw. The ideal spot to slake his carnal desires before making good his escape. He pulled off the worn track into the confines of the draw.

'Why have we turned off here?' Estelle asked in a tremulous voice.

'You'll find out soon enough, missy.' An ugly chuckle left Estelle in no doubt as to the killer's licentious intentions.

She screamed aloud, struggling impotently to throw him off the horse. But Crabbe's left hand held her in a grip of iron. His other struck her a stunning blow across the head.

'Ain't no use calling out,' he snarled. 'There's nobody around to hear you except varmints and buzzards. And they won't help.' He dragged the horse to a halt inside the enclosed defile and pulled the woman off the horse.

'Now let's have us a bit of fun. Reckon I deserve it after all the trouble your damned brother and that sheriff have caused me.' He threw her on to the ground and began unbuckling his gunbelt. An ugly smirking grown sent shivers racing down her spine. 'And you'd be well advised take this quietly, gal, otherwise there'll be a sound leathering to curb your defiance.'

Scrambling backwards on her knees away from the odious predator, Estelle screamed again. Sheer panic lent extra power to her pounding lungs. Crabbe's nauseating response was an ugly chortle as he advanced to take his due.

'No! No! Keep away, you beast!'

Jeff Charnley was following the scent of his trusty hound when he heard the scream split the hot air. The sheepman pricked up his ears. The piercing yell sounded to be of human origin. Or was it merely the cawing of a buzzard in search of its next meal? His brow furrowed in concentration as he drew the roan to a halt and listened intently.

Some of his sheep had strayed towards the scrubby land adjoining that of the Feather Bend. Scruff had picked up their scent and led him to this remote draw. The dog had also picked up on the strangely alien sound. His raggy head flicked to one side. Scruff was an apt name for the unkempt mutt. No hint of any pedigree was evident in the long-haired crossbred mongrel. But he obviously possessed an instinctive nose and a talent for herding sheep.

Again, the nerve-jangling scream shattered the silence. There was no room for doubt. It was clearly a woman's terrified cry for help, coming from over the far side of a low bluff. The dog barked and bounded up the stony slope. He was followed closely by the rider.

The sight that met his gaze was frightening to behold.

A woman was being brutally man-handled by an assailant. It was obvious what he was after. A lurid picture zipped through Jeff's mind as to what his reaction would be had this been his beloved Elsa.

'Leave her alone, mister!' Jeff called out. The attacker immediately paused before his intended lewd assault could be put into action. He turned to face the direction of the command. That was when Jeff recognized the obnoxious Vegas Crabbe.

'I've gotten you eyeballed, Crabbe. Go any further and you're buzzard bait.'

But it was a futile threat. He was only toting an Army Remington revolver converted to cartridge fire. At this distance the only effective response could come from a rifle. Crabbe laughed. He tossed the woman aside and made to lift his own long gun from the saddle boot.

Beside the sheepman his dog growled. Here was the answer to his problem.

'Go Scruff!' Charnley ordered. 'Go get him, boy!'

The dog immediately hurtled off down the back slope. A flying ball of rough hair, he streaked across the intervening stretch. Crabbe stood no chance. He was still trying to lift the rifle to his shoulder when the snarling beast leapt on him. Growling and snapping, the powerful jaws brought the victim crashing to the ground. Man and beast rolled over and over in the dust.

Crabbe screamed. 'Get it off! Get it

off! The critter's tearing me to pieces.'

Sheer panic lent the killer added strength. He managed to throw the snapping hound off, enabling him to draw his revolver. One shot was enough to prevent any further danger. The bullet scored a furrow across Scruff's back. Not a killing shot, it did however give Crabbe time to take proper aim.

Jeff Charnley had spurred his horse down into the draw even as his faithful dog was rolling on the hard ground, whimpering in pain. Seeing his canine companion gunned down and about to be given the final send-off from this scurvy lowlife brought a deep-throated howl of rage from the sheepherder.

Jeff drew his pistol and pumped a full chamber of shells at the rat. Two found their mark. The first clipped the critter's arm, but it was the final slug that dispatched Vegas Crabbe into the netherworld.

Slithering to a halt, Jeff leapt from the saddle. 'You all right, miss?' he inquired breathlessly. A quick nod was all he needed. It was Scruff who needed urgent attention. He gently cradled the wounded animal in his arms. The dog whimpered, nuzzling his cheek and licking him all over his face.

'How is he?' asked Estelle, peering over her saviour's shoulder. A sigh a relief issued from between the man's full lips.

'Look's like it's only a flesh wound. You'll live, won't you, boy?' He stroked the dog's head. 'But that sure was touch and go.'

Jeff aimed a disparaging look at the still form of the late Vegas Crabbe. Then he returned his attention to the woman. 'So what was all that about, miss?'

Estelle briefly related the unpleasant incident at the ranch as far as she was able. In truth she had no real notion as to what had provoked the gunfight.

'I'm just glad that you happened along when you did. I hate to think what would have happened otherwise. That man was . . . well, he . . . '

The woman swallowed. Her face assumed a rosy hue of embarrassment at the very thought of having to explain Crabbe's dissolute intention. Jeff saved her any further discomfiture by inquiring as to where she was from.

'My brother Amos runs the Feather Bend cattle ranch at the top end of the valley. My name is Estelle Crowther.' She held out her dainty hand. The friendly gesture was ignored. Mention of the hated spread brought a sudden cooling of the atmosphere. Charnley sniffed. A snort of derision warped his normally benign countenance into an ugly twist. The woman's brown eyes widened in surprise.

'What have I said?' she exclaimed.

'Maybe you don't know, Miss Crowther,' the sheepman enunciated firmly. 'But your brother and his men tried to run me off my land. When that didn't work, I'm darned sure that he must have somehow blocked the river water.'

Estelle was genuinely shocked to hear of this act of brazen hostility by her own kin. 'I had no idea,' she apologized. 'Why would he do such a thing?'

Charnley laughed. It emerged more as a mocking grunt. 'Maybe you had better ask him that.'

Estelle was not to be thwarted. She scrambled to her feet, a look of defiance obscuring her pretty features.

'I'm asking you, sir.' Her manner was unmistakably determined. Hands on hips she challenged the young man to explain himself. 'You have thrown out these accusations. I want to know why.'

Jeff's aggressive stance softened. He realized that this woman was not to blame. He sighed.

'I'm sorry for blaming you, miss. It just makes me so mad that folks won't accept the idea of cattle and sheep operating together on the same range. My father up in Wyoming is just the same. Cattle and sheep don't mix, and that's the end of it. They're all blinkered in their attitude.'

Estelle was stunned. She was only too well aware of the animosity that sheep caused when they infiltrated cattle country. Perhaps this man was right. But it was no concern of hers. He had saved her from an odious fate and deserved her sympathy.

'If you could escort me back to the ranch, perhaps I can help present your case to my brother. He is the president of the Rio Arriba Cattlemen's Association. It's the least I can do after you saved my reputation from being dishonoured.'

Again she held out a hand as a peace offering. A shy smile creased her Cupid's bow mouth. This time, Jeff accepted.

'It was Scruff here who did all the hard work,' he replied, rubbing the dog's muzzle.

He then mounted up, gently easing the injured animal across his legs. 'We'll have to leave this jigger here,' he added, indicating the bloodied corpse of Vegas Crabbe.

'One of the ranch hands can come back and bury him,' Estelle suggested. She mounted the dead man's horse.

'What's left of him if'n the scavengers don't get here first,' Jeff remarked, casting his shaded eyes skywards.

The girl shivered, then led the way back in the direction of the Feather Bend.

They were halfway to the ranch when they spotted a dust cloud heading their way. Sheriff Toomey emerged from the opaque blur. His face lit up on seeing his sweetheart. The smile vanished instantly when he recognized her companion.

However, his sour regard was softened when Estelle explained how Jeff Charnley had rescued her from the braggart's odious clutches.

'I'm beholden to you, Charnley. I'd never have forgiven myself if anything had happened to Estelle.'

It was clear to the sheepman that the sheriff's concern for the woman amounted to more than just a professional interest. Toomey quickly confirmed their romantic association by kissing the woman's hand.

The dreamy moment was quickly concluded as the sheriff reasserted his official stance.

'Looks like your dog needs some attention.'

'It's him that's the hero of the day,' said Charnley, wishing to maintain some distance between himself and the pro-cattle lawman. 'But his wound is only superficial.'

'In that case I'll bid you good day and escort Estelle back to the ranch.' Toomey made to swing his horse around ready to depart. 'But you'd still do well to heed my warning about your presence around here, mister.'

The sheepman grunted. 'You're barking at the moon if'n you figure I'm gonna quit now, Sheriff.'

The girl held her mount in check. She was taken aback by the rather chilly atmosphere between the two men, rightly assuming it was due to the presence of sheep in the valley. But this young guy and his dog had saved her from a fate worse than death. She was not about to just brush the good deed under the carpet.

'You are welcome at the Feather Bend any time you are in the vicinity, Mr Charnley.' A reproving look at her beau was enough to prevent any further disparaging comment from the lawman. 'Don't hesitate to call on us. And anybody tries to bar your way, they'll have me to answer to.' Her pert nose poked the air in a stiff rebuke for her paramour. Toomey cursed under his breath, knowing that later he would be required to offer up a good deal of contrition.

Jeff Charnley couldn't resist a sly smirk. 'I'm obliged, Miss Crowther. At least there appears to be somebody around here who ain't prejudiced against my flock.'

'Until then, sir,' she said, spurring off. 'And once again, my sincere thanks.'

Toomey did not follow immediately. He nudged his mount over beside the sheepman.

'You'll be glad to hear that the water supply will be back to normal before the day is out. It was Crabbe and his buddies who took it into their heads to shut off the Questa Dam sluice gate. They didn't take kindly to me putting them under arrest. The other two have met the same fate as Crabbe.'

Charnley was less than keen to accept the sheriff's attempt at smoothing things over.

'It would have taken a darned sight more than that to drive me off'n the range. I'm here to stay. So you can tell your pal Crowther that when you see him.'

The sheepman's mule-headed attitude riled the sheriff. 'You're a fool, Charnley, if'n you think that sheep and cattle can mix happily in Rio Arriba. But it's my job to prevent any trouble, even if'n it means saving a lunkhead like you from getting his head blown off.' Tight-lipped, Heck Toomey galloped off after his lady love.

Jeff Charnley's eye burned into the

disappearing back of the stoic lawman.

'A fool, am I?' he rasped aloud to himself. 'We'll see about that. All you ignorant morons have a big surprise coming your way when the rodeo starts. And that goes for my father as well.'

Scruff licked his hand as if in agreement with the stubborn young buck's manner.

'I sure am glad you're on my side, boy. Now let's get you home pronto so's I can tend to that gash.'

7

Rodeo Time

A week passed without any further incident. Nobody had interfered with Jeff Charnley's sheep. Most of the ranchers were fully occupied in making final preparations for the rodeo.

Scruff had quickly recovered from the gunshot wound. Although it did not affect his herding duties, the dog now moved with a slight tilt to the left. Estelle Crowther had called at the spread to check on the animal. The pair had instantly made friends.

She had also made the sheriff suffer for his stiff manner towards the man who had rescued her from the odious clutches of Vegas Crabbe. Her aloof manner was deliberate, intended to make her *inamoratos* fully aware that she was a woman with her own mind.

113

But it was a temporary cooling off. A rapid softening of her starchy demeanour followed after Toomey was forced to consume a mammoth helping of humble pie.

So the day of the rodeo arrived. The town was abuzz with excitement. Well before the start of the show at ten o'clock in the morning the stands were filled to capacity with spectators.

At one end a raised rostrum had been erected, enabling the judges and dignitaries to obtain a clear view of proceedings in the oval arena. At the opposite end was a small enclosure for gentlemen of the press. Reporters representing newspapers from all parts of the territory had gathered. The Chama Rodeo was now a prestigious event that deserved extensive coverage.

At ten on the dot, a whistle was blown and the master of ceremonies welcomed one and all through a megaphone. His speech, however, went on for longer than expected. This was not what the crowd had come for. Listening to Kingpin

Muldoon flexing his jaw muscles was time wasted that should be devoted to the main event.

A restive murmuring from the crowd was cut short by a shouted comment from one of the stands.

'We ain't come here to listen to your burbling, Kingpin. We want some action, don't we boys?'

The remark brought a hail of accord, mingled with laughter and cheers from all parts of the stadium. Muldoon raised his hands.

'OK, gents, I get the message. Just need to get the official business over with first.'

'Rodeoing is the only business we want to see,' was the riposte punched out from another loudmouth. 'Hee-haw, cut the jaw!'

More laughter and stamping of feet, but it was all done in a jovial and good-natured way.

So the master of ceremonies immediately bowed to the audience by satisfying their bluntly delivered request. The first event was announced.

Calf-roping always opened the proceedings. There were six contestants. In a suitably officious voice Kingpin then announced the first entrant.

'And to start off this year's rodeo we have Skip Daley of the Feather Bend. He won the trophy for best calf-roper last year. Think you can do it again, Skip?'

The young cowboy raised his hat to the audience as the calf was released in the arena. A roar burst from a thousand lips.

Straight away he bounded after the yearling. The lariat whirled round above his head. Judging the move to perfection, he flicked the rope at the right moment to bring the animal down. No time was wasted as he leapt off his mustang and quickly tethered the rear legs in the approved manner. In a flourishing finale Skip Daley stood back, waving his hat in the air. Cheering broke out again.

'That was a mighty fine example of calf-roping,' declared the master of ceremonies. 'Don't you think so, folks?' More cheering and waving of flags. 'And your time, Skip, is a remarkable . . . twenty-eight seconds.'

Five more entrants came and went. But none could match Skip Daley's performance. In the stand, Amos Crowther was preening himself on his cowman's performance. The lofty expression flooding his rubicund face told everyone that this cup was in the bag. His supercilious demeanour faded as he heard a sudden announcement by Muldoon.

'It seems that we have a surprising late entry, folks,' the announcer proclaimed, reading from a piece of paper just given to him. 'And it is . . . ' Kingpin's mouth fell open. 'Well, I . . . ' He burbled before recovering his composure. 'Give a warm Chama welcome to . . . Jeff Charnley of the Woollieback spread.'

An ominous silence descended on the gathering as the sheepman rode into the arena. His head was held high, no hat-waving theatrics here. Then an excited muttering rippled through the crowd. Few within the stadium had not heard about the arrival of sheep on their range. Now the man who had brought them to the Arriba country had the effrontery to rate himself on a par with cattlemen.

Harsh discordant laughter broke out among the predominantly cattle-farming gathering. But it lacked any cheeriness. This was a distinctly hostile reception.

'You've got a nerve, muscling in on our show,' grumbled one disgruntled onlooker.

'Who does this jerk think he is?' mocked the spectator sitting next to him. 'Ornery sheep-dipper figuring he can handle beeves.'

'Must have come to the wrong town,' interjected another voice from the opposite side of the arena. Then, bellowing raucously at the mounted figure, he issued some derisive advice:

'Sheep wrangling is over on the Navaho lands, mister. Those durned red devils have sent you down the wrong trail.'

Mocking guffaws burst forth from a myriad throats. Startled by the sudden cacophony, a flock of meadow larks twittered and flew off.

Jeff remained unfazed. It was as if he was alone in the stadium. Slowly, his movements and gestures exhibiting a cool confidence, he circled around waiting for the calf to be released from its pen. Moments later the gate opened and the calf scampered into view. The noise abated as everybody watched, fully expecting an abysmal and humiliating performance from the sheepman.

'Now we'll see what this jasper is really made of,' remarked Amos Crowther, who had joined Sheriff Toomey and his sister on the rostrum. A sneering grunt echoed the views of those around him. 'My betting is that he's way out of his depth. Skip Daley will wipe the floor with him.'

Toomey eyed his associate. The lawman's logical instinct for delving beneath the obvious made him wonder why this guy was entering a cattleman's contest. Charnley was out to prove something.

'Care to make a small wager on that, Amos?' he asked.

Crowther greeted the suggestion with a curled lip. 'Anything you like, Heck.'

'How about ten bucks?'

'Make it fifty.' The rancher smirked. 'No sense in turning down the chance to earn myself some easy dough.'

Toomey nodded and spat on his hand. The two men shook on the deal.

'Easiest dough I ever made,' the rancher chuckled.

The two old pals turned their attention back to the arena as the calf charged across the sandy enclosure with Jeff Charnley in hot pursuit. His lariat twirled once, then flew towards the fleeing beast. The deft manoeuvre had been timed to perfection. Dragging back on the reins, the blue roan knew instinctively what was expected of it. The lariat tightened, bringing the calf to a juddering halt.

Jeff leapt from the saddle and in the bat of an eyelid had tethered the animal in a manner that brought a gasp of surprise from the gathering. Mouths gaped wide. A buzz of startled muttering broke out when Kingpin Muldoon declared that the winner of the calf-roping was Jeff Charnley in a time of twenty-three seconds.

Much to the amusement of Heck Toomey, Crowther was spluttering and gurgling. At last he was able to voice his opinion.

'Had to be a stroke of pure luck. That's it. The guy just scraped through by the skin of his teeth. A fluke. He won't stand a chance in the bull-dogging. My boy Rance Treat has never been beaten.'

An hour later, when all the contestants had wrestled their bulky adversaries to the ground, Muldoon called for there to be quiet as he announced the result.

'A close-run thing, folks. Everybody did well. But the judging panel are agreed that the winner is . . . ' He peered down at the list. 'Once again it's Jeff Charnley.'

'Now what have you to say, Amos?'

chided the sheriff. 'Looks like this guy has all the makings of a good rancher. That bet of your'n is looking a mite shaky.'

Amos could only flap his mouth in amazement. More was to come. Charnley also won the bronc-riding. In the end, when the awards were presented, the sheepman took four of the principal trophies. Milldew Haywain of the Broken Wheel managed to win the wagon dash.

Amos Crowther only managed to win two, sharing the honours with one judged to be a draw. This latter saved him some face. It was in the final event — the horse race. His palomino, Flash, was able to keep pace with Charnley's roan, even taking the lead twice on the triple circuit around the edge of Chama town. It was neck and neck towards the finish line. The dead heat pronounced was a fair result.

But it was left for Jeff Charnley to receive all the accolades.

The unlikely top rider of the rodeo

received the hearty congratulations of the organizers, none of whom were involved in the cattle business.

'In all my years organizing these events up and down the country, I ain't never seen anything like this before,' declared the chief promoter. 'You are to be commended, sir.'

But there were others at the show who were puzzled by the whole thing. How did a sheepman come to be so adept at handing cattle? In the annals of the Chama Rodeo, nothing like this had ever happened before.

That same evening there was a celebration held in the swankiest hotel in town. All the dignitaries were gathered in the Prairie Queen to enjoy the festivities. The name of Jeff Charnley was on everybody's lips. Others had also done well at the show, but it was the sheepman who was the sensation of the whole event.

The enigmatic contestant was more than happy to give interviews to the numerous press reporters.

The eager throng pressed forward,

eager to hear the young man's secret.

'How did you do it, Mr Charnley?' asked one reporter at the front.

Jeff shrugged off the tributes being showered upon him. 'Just good training and a heap of practice is all. Just because I run sheep don't mean I can't handle other animals. But you boys make sure to headline that it was a sheepman that knocked out the cattle kings on their home ground.'

Scribbling pens wrote down his every word, obtaining quotations in support of their narratives. These would be wired back to the respective papers for inclusion in the next editions. This was big news.

'Amos has been like a bear with a sore head,' chuckled Estelle Crowther, snuggling up to her beau at the back of the room. 'He hates being beaten.'

'He ain't too keen on losing a bet neither,' replied Toomey. 'That fifty smackers will put a roof on that new house I'm building out on the flats. Perhaps you would like to come down sometime and select the wallpaper?'

The bashful lawman wasn't quite ready to pop the question. But Estelle could read between the lines. She smiled, a cheeky glint in her eye.

'I'd be glad to, Heck. Perhaps I could also make some suggestions about the sleeping arrangements while I'm there.' Toomey's face blossomed into a setting sun much to her amusement. To save him any further embarrassment, she quickly brought the subject back to the new cock of the walk.

'I'd never have thought it possible that a sheepman could be so skilled when it came to handling cattle.' Estelle's brow furrowed in deep thought. 'It doesn't make any sense.'

The sheriff heaved a sigh of relief at finding himself back on familiar ground. 'I've been wondering about that too,' he agreed, arrowing a quizzical frown at the popular young man from Wyoming. 'There's much more to this guy than meets the eye.'

Once the reporters had dispersed,

one nattily dressed dude sauntered over and drew Jeff to one side. A neatly waxed pencil moustache enhanced the confident manner of a pushy individual used to getting his own way. Tucked into the hatband of his grey derby was a gold press card — an indication that he was from one of the leading newspapers.

'Mind if I have a private word, Mr Charnley,' he whispered in a clandestine manner intended to convey an air of mystery and influence. 'My name is Pierre Dupris. I'm with the *New Orleans Banner*.'

Jeff was intrigued.

'It is clear, sir, that you are a cattle man at heart,' Dupris asserted. A thick accent betrayed his French origins. 'No mere sheepherder could have learnt all those skills, then challenged and beaten experienced cowboys on their own turf.' It was a statement of assumed fact rather than a question. His pen was held at the ready to scribble down Jeff's response.

'I don't wish to comment on that

right now, Mr Dupris. But I have my own reasons for taking these jaspers on.' Jeff was being cagey. He had no wish to have all the details concerning the rift with his father splashed all over the papers. Mention of the Charnley name would be sufficient. 'All I can say is that the answer lies up north in Wyoming.'

'So you are from Wyoming?' the reporter remarked. Jeff nodded. 'Well, it just so happens that my paper has a sister sheet based in Casper. You may have read it — the *Northern Echo*. Would you have any objection to my sending them the story? I can guarantee that it will be front-page news. And naturally a substantial fee will be paid for your cooperation.'

Jeff smiled, his eyes glittering. This was just what he wanted. The money was of no importance. All he wanted were the details of his success as a sheepman in a cattlemen's rodeo to be splashed all over the territory.

'You just make sure to write it up

under the headline I've told you,' was all he said.

'I sure will.' Dupris held out his hand, which Jeff shook. The reporter then hurried away, eager to get the scoop wired off to Casper. With any luck it would be in the next issue, due out later in the week.

Amos Crowther had sidled up beside the sheriff who was standing at the bar on his own. Estelle had left to visit a friend.

Hostile eyes like daggers were boring into the young sheepherder's back. The rancher was bristling with ill-concealed annoyance. Forfeiting his winning status was bad enough, but losing to a sheep-dipper was humiliating. Levelling the issue with the result of the horse race offered little consolation.

The two friends moved closer to hear what was being said.

As Jeff moved away to get some air, his attention was focused solely on the effect the newspaper article would have in Wyoming. The two listeners were ignored. He was muttering under his breath. On passing the sheriff and his companion, the final words were picked up.

' . . . so this will really stick in your craw, Pa. A sheepman getting the better of your breed. Things are shaping up better than I could have expected.'

The two friends looked at one another. 'What in blue blazes did he mean by that?' exclaimed Crowther, scratching his head.

'That guy is no sheepherder. That's for sure,' surmised the sheriff. 'It's all a charade. The guy has a chip on his shoulder bigger than your moustache, Amos. And all this is aimed at his father.'

'What do you reckon it's all about, Heck?' The rancher didn't wait for an answer. The mammoth face-whiskers twitched and bristled with indignation. 'If'n that guy sticks around here strutting his stuff like a blamed peacock, there's gonna be big trouble. My boys are fuming at being licked by the likes of him.'

'Reckon there's only one thing for it,' declared the sheriff, setting his hat straight.

Crowther eyed his friend. 'You gotten a plan, Heck? 'Cos some'n sure needs to be done, and pretty darned quick.'

'I'm heading for Wyoming,' announced Toomey. 'If'n I catch the morning flyer I can link up with the Northern Express at Antonito and be in Casper within three days.' Without further ado he headed off to the station ticket office to book a seat.

'Good luck to you, Heck,' Crowther called after him. Then in a more subdued tone added, 'We're all gonna need a whole passel of good fortune to prevent a range war blowing up when this gets out.'

8

Wyoming Bound

It was a long and tiring journey from Chama north to Casper in Wyoming territory. Four changes of train were needed, each wait adding to Heck Toomey's frustration. During the overnight stopover in Laramie, the New Mexico tinstar introduced himself to the territorial law department to find out more about Jeff Charnley and his mysterious insinuations.

There he learned that the fake sheepman was the only son of the leading rancher in the territory. Rafe Charnley was the well-respected boss of the Flying Arrow in the Big Horn Valley. The nearest town was Casper. And his luck was in. A new branch line had recently opened to service the burgeoning cattle industry.

So that town had to be Heck's destination. From there he could hire a horse and introduce himself to the rancher. Then perhaps he could uncover the truth behind Jeff Charnley's strange behaviour.

Once he had arrived in Casper Heck got himself a room at the National Hotel, then he went to the nearest saloon. The Yellow Dog was right opposite the hotel. It was a good place to begin his inquiries.

His luck was in. After asking at the bar he was immediately directed to a figure sitting alone. Rafe Charnley was hunched over a bottle of rye in the far corner of the room. The rancher was deep in thought. Only the day before he had learned that another group of shepherds had infiltrated the upper end of the Big Horn valley. It was rough pasture, totally unsuited to cattle. But that didn't lighten the ranch owner's lugubrious mood.

Eventually, as sure as eggs is eggs, they'd seek out the more succulent pastures. Where was it going to end? As chairman of the Cattlemen's Association it was his duty to organize some form of resistance. Not until these woolly-backed vermin had been driven off the range could he and the other ranchers rest easy. The level of the liquid in the bottle in front of him dropped further.

Not for the first time he wondered as to the fate of his son. Since their acrimonious blood feud had blown up, he had heard nothing.

The sheriff sauntered across and stood in front of the morose toper.

Charnley hadn't moved a muscle. Only when the newcomer's shadow fell across the table did he deign to raise a weary head. The lawman introduced himself.

'The name is Heck Toomey,' he announced, tapping the silver star pinned to his vest. 'I'm the sheriff of Rio Arriba County in New Mexico.'

'A long way from home, ain't you, Sheriff?' came the somewhat apathetic reply. The rancher didn't even bother to ask what the lawman wanted. Rheumy eyes just stared into an opaque distance.

'It's about your son, Mr Charnley.'

That announcement pricked at the rancher's lethargy. 'What about him?' Toomey's laconic reply had sure collared his attention.

So without further ado, the newcomer got down to business informing the rancher about the trouble that Jeff Charnley was causing within his jurisdiction. The cattleman listened intently, his whole being stiff as a ramrod.

'So that's where the young fool has landed up,' he muttered, knocking back another hefty slug of whiskey. 'What in thunderation is his game — running a damned sheep farm?' He hawked a lump of goo on to the floor.

'Your son is causing me a heap of trouble,' grumbled Heck, accepting a glass. He poured out his own drink. 'It's as clear as daylight that he is a cattleman, born and bred. And you're the only man who can answer your own question, Mr Charnley.' He peered hard at the rancher, waiting for him to open up. 'Best if'n you tell me the whole story.'

The rancher was nonplussed. It took him a moment and another shot to compose his thoughts before he began relating the events that had led to the family feud.

'I've since found out that he was seeing a girl from the sheep farm that caused all the hoo-ha. A son of mine cavorting with some sheep gal don't bear thinking on.' The bitterness in the words expressed all his pent-up abhorrence for the hated interlopers. 'But the thing I can't figure is what he's trying to prove by taking up with them blamed creatures down in your neck of the woods. It don't make no sense.'

Heck quickly assimilated Charnley's version of the events. His analytical mind, which had helped him to net a host of lamebrain lawbreakers, sifted through the guy's heavily biased account. He reached the conclusion that both father and son were stubborn critters unable to comprehend each other's point of view.

Now that he had the facts at his disposal the sheriff felt confident that he could persuade the young hothead to curtail his reckless quest for revenge.

'He's putting his life and those of a lot of others in danger by blatantly antagonizing everybody in Rio Arriba,' he told Rafe Charnley. 'Now that I know what it's all about, I'm sure that he can be made to see the error of his ways and come back home. Maybe the two of you can then settle your differences amicably.'

'I sure hope so. I never wanted a split like this.' Charnley's hard demeanour slipped. Another gulp of hard liquor disappeared down his throat. 'Jeff belongs up here with me on the Flying Arrow.'

Heck nodded in wholehearted agreement. Mule-headedness made folks intolerant, unable to see both sides of an argument and this was the result.

Unless some sort of compromise was reached, nothing up here was likely to change. He shook his head in exasperation. Charnley didn't notice. He was in the right, and that was that.

'I'm heading back tomorrow,' the lawman concluded, getting to his feet. 'I'll wire you how I get on after talking to your son. Whatever happens though, he has to be stopped before this disastrous situation gets out of hand.'

The one thing that Heck Toomey had failed to appreciate was that the press coverage of the rodeo was not restricted to New Mexico. He was unaware of the conversation that had taken place between Jeff Charnley and the French reporter at the end of the rodeo.

Even as the two men were discussing the matter, the printing press in the office of the *Northern Echo* was churning out the next edition of the paper. There on the front page was the eye-catching headline dictated by Jeff Charnley.

★   ★   ★

Later that day four men burst into the Yellow Dog. They were waving copies of the newspaper in the air and sniggering to each other. The sight of Rafe Charnley in the corner elicited a bout of hearty guffaws.

The rancher looked up. His face assumed a dark glower of hate. Sheep-dippers. And in a cattleman's saloon.

'What the heck . . . ?' he blurted out.

He was given no opportunity to voice his displeasure at their presence. The leader of the group was none other than Joachim Fallenborg. He was accompanied by his son Sven and two other sheepmen from the neighbouring valley. He strode purposefully over to the rancher and threw the paper down on the table.

'Guess you ain't seen this, Charnley,' he said, confronting the rancher. An arrogant sneer was pasted across his thin features. The other men jostled forward, eager to join in with the barracking. For once it was their turn to have the upper hand. 'That son of your'n is a right turncoat, ain't he just?'

Sven piped up with his own ribald comment. 'Fancy a cattleman turning to sheep then hoodwinking his own kind.'

'And thrashing the critters in a rodeo on their own turf. Don't that beat all?' added another jubilant herdsman.

'Haw! Haw! Haw!' The coarse laughter echoed around the room. 'You'll never live this down, Charnley,' added Sven Fallenborg. 'We'll see to that.'

The sheepmen paraded off, keen to spread the word around Casper. When he'd read the article, Charnley was seething with rage.

'How dare that cocky upstart humiliate me like this. When word gets out, I'll be the laughing-stock of the whole territory.' He threw the paper down and stamped on it. 'He's not going to get away with this. I'll make darned certain of that. I'll make that turncoat pay big time for shaming his own flesh and blood in this manner.'

With the taunts of the shepherds

ringing in his ears, Charnley lurched out of the saloon. Any notion that the visiting New Mexico sheriff would sort out the situation was forgotten. An insult of this magnitude demanded action of a much more vigorous nature. He knew exactly where that could be found.

Quickly shrugging off some of the effects of the rye whiskey, he set his hat and necktie straight and headed off down the street. Two blocks down, he forked off the main drag down a narrow alley between the butcher's shop and a flower-seller. The blend of contrasting odours did not make for a pleasant ambience. A threatening growl forced him to veer away from a snarling mutt, which was chewing on a large bone.

'You're welcome to it,' mumbled the still half-soused rancher.

At the back end of the passage was an isolated drinking den with the decidedly whimsical name of the Lotus Flower. Charnley didn't bother to knock on the door.

Barging straight in, he was confronted

by four men playing cards. Three others were lounging against a bar nursing tankards of beer. They all bore the grizzled appearance of cold-blooded desperadoes. They eyed the intruder with curled lips and ill-concealed annoyance. Only a fool or someone in desperate need of their six-shooting skills would be foolhardy enough to interrupt a weekly poker session.

A long-haired bruiser by the name of Wildcat Mancos lurched to his feet, grabbing for his shooter. The leader of the pack stayed his edgy reflexes.

'It's OK, Wildcat,' Snag LaBone placated his sidekick, pushing him back into his seat. 'This is Mr Charnley. He's a friend of mine who owns the biggest cattle spread in the territory. We've had dealings before.' He didn't elaborate.

The tough guy's laid-back manner needled Charnley, but he retained a cool head. LaBone cast a thoughtful eye on the newcomer, who was rightly sensing that his hidden talents were being sought.

Since the shooting on the ranch, the hired gunslinger had spent most of his time in Casper. His reputation as a hired gunslinger had attracted numerous ne'r-do-wells. Charnley had kept him on a retainer for just such an occasion as this. But the rancher's sudden appearance had resurrected memories of the demeaning incident involving his son. They did not sit well.

'So what is it you want, Charnley?' he snapped.

'Howdie, Snag. I have a job for you that involves a little erm . . . gentle persuasion.' The rancher's sly smirk was accompanied by a brief signal to follow him outside.

LaBone handed his cards to Bulldog Lannigan. 'Make sure you don't throw this away,' he warned the heavyweight bruiser while grinning at the others. The odious leer was intended to throw his opponents off their guard. In truth, he was playing a classic poker bluff. 'I have a sizeable pot running on this hand.'

Lannigan played along with the

pretence. 'Don't worry, boss,' he sniggered. 'You can depend on me.'

Then LaBone followed the rancher out into the alley, resuming a blasé manner.

'So what's this all about?' asked the hired gun, who was intrigued despite his nonchalant attitude.

'I need you to head down to Chama in New Mexico. My son has started up a sheep ranch down there, hoping to show me up.'

LaBone couldn't resist a ribald chortle. 'I read about that in the *Echo*. I can see why you might be a tad miffed.'

Charnley's eyes blazed. 'This ain't no laughing matter. Do you want this job?'

'Sure, sure,' the hardcase backtracked. 'No offence meant. Just seems mighty strange, is all, that he should pull a stunt like that.'

'Well, listen up then!' the rancher snapped. 'I want you to make certain that Jeff regrets what he's done by burning him out.' LaBone's eyes widened. Charnley extracted two cigars from his jacket pocket and handed one to the gunman. They both lit up. 'But I don't want him hurt. Do it properly and his reason for being down there will be destroyed. That should force the young pup to come back up here with his tail between his legs.'

LaBone blew out a perfect smoke ring before answering. He clicked his tongue. 'Sounds like a pretty serious undertaking to me. One that's gonna cost you.'

'I'm willing to pay you five thousand: half up front, the rest when the job's done.'

The gang boss threw back his head and chortled loudly. 'Five grand?' huffed LaBone. 'That ain't much. Don't forget I have expenses — and my boys to pay off.'

Charnley gritted his teeth. He hated being bulldozed. And by a skunk like Snag LaBone to boot, which made it doubly repellent. But what choice did he have? His fists bunched in frustration, his florid features blotching angrily.

'No need to get so touchy, Rafe,' LaBone chided, slapping the rancher on the shoulder. 'If'n you want a good job doing, money should be no object. Ain't that so?' The oily smile was akin to that of a sidewinder eyeing up its next meal.

Charnley balked at the over-familiarity and use of his first name. But he forced himself to remain taciturn. Following a moment's hesitation, his restrained nod of agreement released the tense atmosphere. 'I'll up it to eight grand. And that's my last offer. Take it or leave it.'

'That's more like it. And you can depend on me and the boys to do a first-rate job.'

They shook hands to clinch the deal.

'The important thing is to make sure you don't lay a finger on Jeff. Otherwise the deal's off. Got that?'

LaBone's shoulders lifted in a lazy gesture of accord. 'You're the boss. And you have the word of Snag LaBone that not a finger will be laid on the kid. But the farm will be well and truly routed.'

He grinned, exposing a row of uneven teeth yellowed by too much baccy-chewing. 'It's as good as done.'

Charnley then extracted a billfold from his jacket and pealed off a wad of greenbacks which he handed over. LaBone's greedy peepers glazed over as he flicked through all that lovely dough before stuffing it into his pocket.

And with that assurance, Rafe Charnley departed, satisfied that within weeks he and his son would be reunited.

9

Bad News

Sheriff Heck Toomey was at the railroad depot early the next morning to catch the southbound train for Denver. He was checking the timetable when a group of seven riders trotted past. Leading them was Snag LaBone. The sheriff paid them no heed, assuming they were cowboys just passing through.

The gang boss was not about to lay out good money for a train journey. It would take them a good week to reach New Mexico by the direct route south through mountain country. But he was in no hurry. As they passed by one of the bunch drew his horse to a halt and eyed the lawman's broad back.

Dirty Dick Shifter's face creased up. The sluggish brain was turning over.

147

The desperado prided himself on never forgetting a face. He knew that guy from someplace. But where? He scratched the knife scar on his cheek. Then it came to him. His fingers snapped as the penny dropped.

Dodge City! And that critter was Heck Toomey, the starpacker who had run him out of town for the minor offence of shooting up the Long Branch one night. Shifter had just come up the Chisholm Trail with a herd of 2,000 longhorns from the Panhandle ranch. Along with the rest of the crew who had been paid off, they were all intent on having a good time.

Everything was going fine until they reached the Long Branch. A rival crew began shouting disparaging comments regarding the sexual prowess of the Panhandle boys. The other cowboys gave as good as they received in the verbal exchange. It was the usual *mine's bigger than yours* sort of badinage.

But Dirty Dick was having none of it. Three types of heavy drinkers can be identified by the observant onlooker. Firstly there are those who become quietly downbeat after downing a skinful; then we have the jovial good-time slap-on-the-back fellas always ready with a joke and quip; and lastly there are the troublemakers, those who feel that every man's hand is against them. Shifter would normally have been in the first category, except when he became riled up. This was just such an occasion.

Without warning, he drew his revolver and shot one of the culprits of the opposing faction. Luckily the bullet only nicked the guy's arm. But it was enough to see everybody diving for cover. As it happened, Marshal Heck Toomey chose that moment to enter the saloon on one of his nightly check-ups when cowboys were in town. His brusque order to Dirty Dick to put up his pistol was ignored. Instead Shifter decided to vent his spleen on the lawman.

It was a mistake that was to cost him dear.

★ ★ ★

A snarl of vengeance illuminated the tough's grizzled features. His growl of anger had been heard by the others, who now pulled up. Shifter drew his pistol, intending to repay his long-held grudge against Toomey.

Seeing his plans being placed in jeopardy, LaBone grabbed his associate's arm.

'Cut out the fireworks, you durned fool,' he upbraded the angered Dirty Dick. 'Kill a lawman and we'll have the whole territory hunting us down.'

'He was the rat who made a laughing stock of me in Dodge back in '74,' complained Shifter. 'I swore to get even.'

'You want revenge? OK by me,' growled LaBone, forcing himself to remain calm. 'But not until we've done this job and been paid off. Savvy?' His firm hand squeezed the tough's arm. His threatening glower was enough to force his subordinate into backing down. LaBone had not become the boss through pussyfooting around. 'You hear me, Dick? Crazy stunts like that will ruin everything.'

The gritty aside had been uttered in a harsh whisper. The hardcase had no desire to draw any unwelcome attention to their task. Shifter knew better than to argue the toss. Others who had opposed LaBone's blunt authority were now resting in various Boot Hill cemeteries across the West. He quickly simmered down.

Once the wayward thug had been brought into line, the boss called out stridently, 'OK boys, let's ride. It's a long way to Chama.'

It was an innocent enough remark that La Bone had let slip. He had no inkling of Heck Toomey's association with the New Mexico township. That was a detail Rafe Charnley had failed to pass on, or had not considered relevant. And now, unwittingly, the gang boss had gone against his own order and let the cat out of the bag.

The sheriff was instantly placed on his guard.

Why in blue blazes were those jaspers heading for his bailiwick in New Mexico? The leader's revelation was far too specific to be a coincidence. There had to be more to it. The obvious conclusion was that the apparently throwaway disclosure was related to his meeting with Charnley.

There was only one way to find out if his suspicions had any foundation.

The train was forgotten. He could always catch a later one. The livery barn was at the far end of town. He hurried off to hire himself a horse. Five unwary riders should be a cinch to trail. But Heck knew that he would need to wait until nightfall when they stopped to make camp before he could discover what nefarious scheme was being hatched. With that in mind he paid a call at the general store to pack in some basic provisions.

Keeping the gang under surveillance proved as easy as he had figured. He soon caught them up. A blind man could follow the trail. There was no reason for the gang to suspect they were being followed. Heading east of south, they followed the valley of the Medicine Bow, which was confirmation enough for Toomey that he had not misheard the leader's unguarded remark.

It was around dusk when the gang made camp by a creek fringed by dwarf willows. Heck hauled rein and waited until darkness had enveloped the landscape in its umbrageous cloak before making his move. Ground-hitching the hired chestnut, he crept through the tree cover, making sure to create no noise that would alert the gang to an alien presence. Only the odd scuffling of night creatures and the creak of swaying branches disturbed the deceptive tranquillity.

A flicker of light up ahead pointed unerringly to the campsite. Inching ever closer, Toomey soon reached an open sward where he paused. Six shadowy figures were sprawled around the dancing flames on which a black coffee pot sat. One man was idly stirring a concoction in another pan while two others fed the line of picketed horses. LaBone was sitting alone, smoking a cigar. He held out his mug for it to be filled with hot coffee before adding a snort of whiskey from a hip flask.

Unless the hovering watcher drew closer, it would be impossible to hear what they were saying. All he could pick up was a rough murmur interspersed with various guffaws. The smell of pinto beans and strong Arbuckles informed Heck's stomach that he had not eaten all day. He stifled a rumbling gurgle that threatened to emerge in a burst of wind. Revealing his presence through such a discharge would have been exceedingly embarrassing in other circumstances. Out here it could prove deadly.

After allowing his innards to settle, the lawman slithered closer to hear what was being discussed. He had to wait until the men had finished their meal and lighted up before the leader revealed his own plans.

They had nothing to do with what Rafe Charnley had instructed.

The men had been discussing how they intended spending their individual split of the pay-out once the job was completed. After LaBone had pocketed the lion's share, plus an extra slice dubiously labelled 'expenses', that left his men with around 800 bucks apiece. Enough for a few months' carousing. That was when LaBone spoke up. His voice easily carried to the hidden spy.

'How would you boys like to have a much bigger payday?' he proposed, rolling a cigarillo around his fleshy lips. 'The sort that would see you living in clover until the cows come home.'

That proposal certainly caught their attention. Greedy peepers eyed the boss.

'What's on your mind, Snag?' asked a wary guy called Fishtail Emery.

'I never turn down a chance to make easy money,' remarked his close buddy.

Diminutive Charlie Twist was whittling a piece of wood into the shape of a revolver with his trademark Bowie knife. An insignificant little runt, Twist had killed more men than any of the others. All with the help of his razor-edged friend.

LaBone sucked hard on the thin tube of tobacco before answering. He enjoyed holding centre stage.

'Charnley wants us to wreck his kid's chances of making a go of sheepherding down Chama way. His orders are to wipe out the farm. But he don't want us to touch the boy. That way he figures the kid will crawl back home to rejoin his doting pappy.' The leader eyed the watching faces, enjoying their curiosity before continuing. 'And if nothing else, Snag LaBone is a man of his word.'

Puzzled frowns skewered the gang boss as the others listed intently.

'Well, boys, we're gonna do just that. But in a way he'd never expect. By shooting him dead we won't be breaking our promise, will we? And at the same time, we'll be doing our bounden duty to rid the West of those woolly-backed vermin.'

Emery posed the question to which the grim answer was etched on to more than one leathery face.

'How is that gonna net us any kind of bonanza, boss? We'd still be hauled up before a judge for murder.'

'And that's a sure-fire invitation to a necktie party I don't want to accept,' intervened the sceptical growl of Wiley Dobbs.

LaBone was expecting such a display of dissension. He merely smiled. It emerged as an evil leer.

'You boys reckon I ain't got all that figured out?' He chuckled uproariously and added another liberal slug of liquor to his coffee. 'That's why I'm bossing this outfit and you guys are the gofers. You see . . . ' His voice had dropped to a mysterious whisper. Toomey was forced to edge closer to catch his drift. ' . . . when Charnley threatens to cause a ruckus, the seven of us will swear blind that we were just obeying his orders. Should he foolishly try to shop us, his neck will be in for a stretching as well. Not even a hothead like him would be that stupid.'

The gang leader allowed the import of this revelation to sink in before concluding, 'We could hold it over the clown for as long as we liked, and he'd have no choice but to pay up on demand. They call it blackmail in legal circles. I call it good business.'

Toomey was stunned, horrified by what he had heard. His mouth flopped open. Now he knew for certain what game these turkeys were playing. And, like all such lowlife scum, they were intent on altering the rules to suit their own despicable ends. An act of sabotage had rapidly degenerated into the major crime of murder. That was obviously a ploy that Charnley could never have anticipated. The lawman snarled. Rats could never be trusted not to bite the hand that fed them.

Another puzzling notion struck the silent spectator.

Something must have bugged the Flying Arrow boss sufficiently after their meeting to make him seek help from these treacherous brigands. But what? He had no idea that news of Jeff Charnley's actions in Chama had become so widespread and that the local sheepmen had become involved.

Swift action was needed to thwart the LaBone Gang's repulsive scheme. Now that he knew the lie of the land, the sheriff had to figure out how to tackle the issue. He was sorely tempted to challenge the heinous crew. A searching hand gripped the butt of his trusted Colt .45. The gun half-rose from its holster.

But seven against one were mighty stiff odds that even a tough lawman like Heck Toomey was loath to tackle. One or two might be taken down, but the others would surely win the uneven contest. Reluctantly he bowed to the inevitable and with the greatest care, crawled back to where he had tethered his cayuse. Leading the animal away from the camp, he did not mount up until well clear.

All thoughts of food had disappeared as he urged the chestnut to a full gallop. There was no time to be lost in apprising that knuckle-headed rancher of the grim course of events he had so unwittingly set in motion.

Yet even a robust dude like Heck Toomey could not keep going for ever. Half an hour later he was visibly wilting. His head was nodding with fatigue. Grudgingly, but for his own survival, the lawman pulled off the trail and made camp. Continue much further and he would have fallen out of the saddle. He was too bushed even to gather kindling for a fire. So a cold camp had to suffice. But he made the best of it with some sticks of beef jerky and an apple and cinnamon pie.

A fine Havana cigar helped ease away the aches of the journey.

Much as he would have preferred to continue onward to the Flying Arrow ranch, the sandman was calling. Toomey found it impossible to resist the sleep-inducer's hypnotic allure. Wrapped in a blanket and warmed by thoughts of the lovely Estelle, he fell into a deep sleep.

The howling of a coyote woke him just after dawn.

Much refreshed, he was soon back in the saddle and once more hurtling north across the rolling grasslands of the Medicine Bow valley. The rest had done him a heap of good. So he was able to make swift progress, crossing the divide around noon by way of a mountain pass known as the Devil's Gate. Thereafter it was a simple case of descending gradually into the southern end of the Big Horn country.

The first traveller he encountered was able to direct him to the Flying Arrow ranch of Rafe Charnley.

He was knocking on the door of the impressive ranch house by late afternoon. The door was opened by a small Chinaman sporting a long black pigtail. The little man bowed and asked his business in a lilting singsong cadence that cracked a rare smile on the lawman's craggy façade.

'Is Mr Charnley at home? Sheriff Heck Toomey needs to speak with him urgently,' the lawman announced firmly.

At that moment Charnley appeared from a side room. The sheriff wasted no time in informing the rancher of his findings. Charnley was noticeably shocked. The blood drained from his face. He would have fallen down had not the little Chinaman briskly stepped forward to support him. Exhibiting surprising strength, he almost carried the pale and shaken rancher into his office and sat him down.

'You sit here, boss, while Lee Fong gets brandy.'

The tough rancher nodded. 'And one for the sheriff too,' he muttered. 'He looks as drained as me.' Toomey was not about to refuse. A slug of French brandy would give them both a much-needed lift.

Glass in hand, the rancher bowed his head in anguish. 'This is terrible,' he wailed. 'All I wanted was to frighten the kid so he would come back home. Now this. I ought never to have trusted a skunk like Snag LaBone. But when those accursed sheepmen burst into the saloon laughing and making me look a fool, it turned my head. I just wanted to punish Jeff for his malicious vindictiveness.'

'It'll be a darned sight more terrible for him if'n LaBone and his men have their way,' snapped Toomey.

'What can I do to stop them?' asked the distraught rancher.

The sheriff had been giving this conundrum a deal of consideration on the long ride back to the Big Horn.

'I'm heading back to Chama on the first train out tomorrow morning,' he declared in a thoughtful manner. 'You get your business sorted out here, then catch the next one in three days' time. On horseback, it will take LaBone at least a week to reach New Mexico. He's not expecting any trouble so won't be in any hurry. That ought to give you enough time to get down there and be waiting to stop those killers doing their worst.'

'I — I don't think LaBone will listen to me now,' Charnley lamented. 'Not with six other men at his disposal. You gotta help me, Sheriff,' the fretful rancher pleaded.

'I'll do what I can to protect you.' Toomey's brusque manner indicated his lack of sympathy for the rancher's plight, which he judged to be of his own making. 'But this is all your and your son's doing. And my responsibility is primarily to the citizens of Rio Arriba County. You'd better hope your skills of persuasion are well honed.'

Not a vindictive man at heart, Toomey's tough stance now softened. Charnley clearly loved his son and bitterly regretted the rift that had blown up between them. Nevertheless, he was still a cattleman underneath. Knowing his son had openly embraced the sheep faction was hard to stomach.

'I'll do everything I can to persuade

Jeff of the foolishness of maintaining this blood feud. Not to mention the ill-feeling it's causing among the cattlemen.' Toomey was well aware that it would be an uphill struggle. His main concern was to keep the peace. If Jeff Charnley continued on the path he had set, he shuddered to think what would happen.

Range wars had broken out for much less provocation in other territories. Heck Toomey was damned if it was going happen in his precinct.

10

Fateful Decision

The Flying Arrow boss made sure he was on the next train heading out of Casper. Curly Bob Spendler had been left in charge to keep things ticking over until his return. Although when that might be was in the lap of the gods.

First stop after the southbound Flyer had crossed over the Colorado border into New Mexico was Pagosa Springs. A wooden maintenance hut adjoining a large water tower were the only features of the remote enclave. This was where the locomotive's boiler could be replenished. A log flume carried water from the Questa Dam which kept the tower at full capacity. That was yet another piece of resourceful engineering that Amos Crowther had initiated. Not only did it provide an essential service to the railroad, it had netted the rancher a regular income.

Rafe Charnley had noticed the sign at the side of the railway announcing their entry into New Mexico. Like many of the other passengers, he stepped down to stretch his legs. Noticing the engineer filling up the boiler, he strolled across.

'Is this halt anywhere near a sheep farm,' he inquired. 'It's run by a guy called Jeff Charnley. Do you know him?'

The engineer chortled. 'Everybody in the territory knows about that guy. You must be a stranger not to have heard that he took on the best cattlemen in the southwest and beat them in the rodeo?' Charnley gritted his teeth as the jovial locomotive driver prattled on. 'Gee, I don't know how he did it. But there were some red faces around when he lifted most of them prizes . . . '

Charnley's irritation threatened to bubble over as another bout of chuckling emerged from beneath the loco man's greasy peaked cap.

'I ain't bothered about that,' he rapped acidly, cutting short the engineer's annoying blether. 'Just tell me how to get there.'

The man ceased his warbling, a piqued eye fastening on to the speaker. Shrugging his shoulders, the man then pointed a languid arm across a stretch of open country.

'Take a walk to the top of yonder butte and you'll be able to see his boundary fence. The ranch ain't no more than a five-mile walk from here. But it's rough country if'n you're thinking of heading off that way.'

That was exactly what was in Rafe Charnley's mind.

Due to a breakdown in Laramie, the train had been delayed for two days until a fresh locomotive could be brought up from Cheyenne. That had inevitably meant that his other connections had been thrown into disarray. Consequently, he was now three days behind schedule. Enough time for

LaBone and his men to have already arrived. Even now he could well be carrying out his dreadful plan.

A more considered reflection of the notion to head across country soon brought home all the drawbacks. Charnley was in a quandary. Common sense told him to stay on the train and head for Chama, where he could contact Sheriff Toomey. The sheriff would be expecting him. A wire from Denver had informed Toomey of the delay. The train would reach the terminus by nightfall.

With no range gear other than an overnight bag, he was ill-equipped for a walking trek. And, apart from a small up-and-over Derringer, he was unarmed.

But the rancher was in a state of panic. Staying on the train would eat up more time. Another day would have passed. Time enough for his son's life to have been snuffed out. A myriad sinister thoughts were spinning round inside his head with the speed of a mad carousel.

What should he do?

Five miles wasn't that far. Set off now

and he ought to make it easily within a couple of hours. His big head nodded vigorously. Jeff was his number one priority now. His son's life was at stake. A firm resolve burning in his heart, the rancher hurried back to the car and climbed aboard to retrieve his small bag.

He jumped back down on to the track and immediately set off for the low butte indicated by the engineer.

Railroad Bill was just climbing back into the cab when he noticed the stumbling figure heading away from the train. 'Hold up there, mister!' he called in a startled cry. 'Surely you ain't thinking of venturing into this terrain on foot and in those duds? That's plumb loco. You're asking for trouble.'

But Charnley ignored the anxious warning. The decision had been made. No amount of cajoling or threats would change his mind now. He would play the hand until the final call.

The engineer shrugged his shoulders, shaking his head. 'Crazy galoot!' he muttered, ambling back to climb into the cab. 'It'll be your funeral.'

This sceptical aside from a distinctly dubious Railroad Bill failed to reach the ears of Rafe Charnley. Not that it would have made the slightest difference to his ill-founded judgement. The guy's blinkered, ornery attitude had once again reared its ugly head.

Bill pulled down hard on the engine's steam whistle to express his disapproval of the rash endeavour. A mournful hoot floated on the breeze announcing the imminent departure of the Flyer.

The plaintive wail induced a family of prairie dogs to emerge from underground. Curious eyes watched as the iron horse trundled away across the plains. The solitary biped in their midst received a more careful scrutiny. Not until they were sure that he was just a passing interloper did the furry beasts return to their burrows.

The chuffing monster, smoke billowing from its balloon stack, slowly pulled away from Pagosa Springs. Startled looks were clearly etched on numerous faces pressed against the car windows as they watched, opened-mouthed, as the greenhorn trekker wandered off into the wilderness.

Charnley paused. He had given little if any thought to the pitfalls of making what had at first appeared to be a simple cross-country stroll. Now, left alone in this wild terrain, a dubious expression beneath his furrowed brow, he pondered on whether he had made the right decision.

More used to the rolling grasslands of Wyoming, he had failed to take account of the rough broken-up mesa country of this southern territory.

The train gathered speed. Too late for regrets now. The die was cast.

Turning his back on the disappearing line of cars, he set his course towards the stony top of the butte. It was a much steeper clamber than he had thought. Only halfway up and he had already stumbled twice, ripping his trousers at the knee. A trickle of red from the torn flesh did not augur well. Another thoughtful look towards the disappearing train, now merely a smudge of white smoke on the horizon, was quickly thrust aside.

He had made his bed. Determination to succeed would assuredly see him through without mishap.

At the crest of the butte he paused again to draw breath. Suddenly it dawned on his mushy brain that he was out of shape. Too many large dinners at the Cattlemen's Club and not enough exercise were quickly beginning to explain the swelling girth beneath the expensive blue suit. He tore off the neck tie and undid his shirt collar.

Panning the expansive vista, all he could see was a never-ending sprawl of rugged mesas criss-crossed by steep ridges and deep valleys. In between, dry grasslands dominated by sagebrush, mesquite and cholla cactus prevailed. Yucca plants bearing white flowers also flourished. Overhead, meadow larks and jays flitted here and there, immune to the stark reality of the unforgiving terrain.

Much as his narrowed gaze tried focusing on the distant horizon, he could see no sign of the boundary fence mentioned by Railroad Bill. Perhaps it had been originally spotted further down the line. But how far? Now that he was cast afoot, it could take hours to find.

Girding himself for the fray, Charnley set off down the back slope. Within a half-hour he had discarded his travel bag and top coat. Sweat was pouring down his face. The silk shirt was already a sodden rag. He soon came upon a rocky canyon. Luckily there was a small creek threading a winding path down the centre which provided some much needed liquid sustenance. He made his way down the side of the canyon.

But the deep rift was heading in the wrong direction. Being a cattleman, Charnley was able to check his direction from the angle of the sun. He had no choice but to head west, hoping that eventually the canyon would split or deviate towards the southerly course he required. It proved to be a futile aspiration.

Another hour passed with no sign of any change in direction. Panic was beginning to grip the ageing rancher's guts. The hot sun was shifting inexorably towards the western horizon. Much more of this and he would be in dire straits. Being cast adrift in this wilderness did not bear thinking on.

Taking the bull by the horns, he launched himself up a narrow stone-choked gully. It was a tough and remorseless ascent. But sheer desperation forced him onwards and upwards. Two steps up, one back. By the time he eventually clambered out on to the flat ledge above, his heart was pounding like a Commanche war drum.

The footslogger's shattered body slumped to the ground, where he lay, sucking in huge gulps of air. For ten minutes he didn't move, staring up at the unbroken azure firmament. Eventually he forced his tired limbs back into motion.

Three vultures perched on the dead branch of desiccated pine stared at him. He could almost see their beaks clucking greedily. He shivered at the thought of providing their next meal.

Stay here and he would surely die.

Slowly he lurched to his feet. Screwed up, his eyes stared towards the south. And there it was — a fence line. He estimated it to be a good three miles distant, and there was a heap of broken country in between to impede his progress. But at least he now had a homing beacon to aim for.

The intervening terrain was a series of shallow but steep-sided gullies carved out by some ancient river system. Negotiating these meandering arroyos proved to be the most taxing phase of the trek which Charnley now bitterly regretted having undertaken. The intervening stretches were choked with waist-high stands of thorny mesquite and buffalo grass.

As the sun disappeared over the distant line of hills, the trekker knew that he would have to spend the night

176

out here. Not only that, dark clouds were quickly gathering. Large banks of menacing thunderheads scudded across the landscape, swallowing up the bright sunlight.

Within minutes the first droplets of rain hit the hard dry ground. Sharp flashes of lightning crackled in the louring sky as a stiff wind hurtled down the arroyo, shredding the cloud banks into grey strips. The awesome jolts were followed soon after by a harsh thunderclap that rumbled like a belching giant.

A flash storm was clearly gathering strength over the Questa Mountains. Stumbling along the arroyo, Charnley desperately sought out somewhere to shelter.

In this luck was with him. A small cave tucked into the north side of the steep banking some six feet off the floor offered a modicum of respite. He was only just in time to avoid a drenching from the sudden downpour.

Within a half-hour the gully was filled with churning muddy water. Charnley gave thanks to his Maker for providing the welcome refuge as the tumbling cascade thrashed and bubbled in angry turmoil. The rancher shivered. A numbing chill wrapped itself around his body, as much due to fear of his exposed predicament as to its actual temperature.

Hunkering down in the back of the cave, he settled himself to wait out the storm. Somehow, amidst the cacophonous ferment, he managed to fall asleep. Sheer exhaustion had claimed his whacked frame.

★   ★   ★

Heck Toomey met the Flyer later that day when it finally puffed into the terminal at Chama. He was waiting on the platform, eagerly scanning the passengers as they disembarked. But there was no sign of Rafe Charnley. As the last one collected his luggage and headed for the hotel, Toomey's brow wrinkled in frustration. He wasn't particularly concerned. A wire sent by the rancher and received from Denver a few days before had informed him about all the delays.

Guess he'll be on the next train, he muttered under his breath. It was still a nuisance. But there was nothing he could do about it now. Another train was not due from up north for three days. The lawman did not want to hire a posse to tackle the LaBone gang until they arrived. Paying a holding fee would not go down well with the town council.

He ambled back to his office twiddling his thumbs at this exasperating setback. Then his logical mind clicked into action. There was one thing he could do. He hooked out a gold-plated hunter watch from his vest pocket. A brief nod sealed his decision. There was still time to set the first part of his plan into motion before sundown. His granite-hard features were set in tenaciously dogged resolve as he headed down to the livery barn.

Next morning, the sheriff was enjoying his usual breakfast at the Rib-Eye Diner when Railroad Bill wandered in.

He was still clad in his blue and white overalls complete with a peaked cap adorned with the Cumbres-Toltec badge. The diner was quite full. Being an affable character, the sheriff motioned for Bill to join him.

'Much obliged, Sheriff,' the older man responded, acknowledging the civil gesture. 'I've been working on the Flyer all night and sure am bushed. One of the piston housings was leaking steam so I had to reseal it.' He stretched his arms, yawning. 'A railroad engineer's work is never done. My stoker is firing her up right now in readiness for an early start.'

Toomey forked a mouthful of fried potatoes into his mouth and indicated with a nod of the head for the loco man to help himself to the coffee while his order was being prepared.

'I was expecting a guy off the Flyer yesterday,' the sheriff said. 'But he didn't show. Now I gotta wait until Thursday.'

Bill sipped his coffee. 'Strange thing happened to me yesterday at Pagosa

Springs.' He paused as the waitress laid down a large plate of bacon and eggs in front of him. Tired eyes bulged. The sight of the delicious repast drove any further thoughts from his head. The inner man was calling, and he was not to be denied.

Waiting until the engineer had taken a few mouthfuls, Toomey then casually inquired about the occurrence at Pagosa Springs.

'Yep,' the engineer averred, forking at a piece of bacon. 'Mighty strange.' His lined face creased up on recollecting the bizarre event. Toomey waited, impatience evident on his frowning visage.

'This guy asked about the whereabouts of the Charnley place.' At the mention of the sheepherder, the sheriff's whole body stiffened. 'I told him where to find it. Then, without another word, he upped sticks and set off across country. I tried telling him to wait until we reached Chama. But he wouldn't listen. The guy was intent on getting over there fast. Last I saw he was heading south on foot.'

'Was he a big dude, well-dressed, around fifty with a clipped moustache waxed at the ends?' asked the animated lawman.

Bill nodded. 'That's the fella. You expecting him?'

Suddenly the grim import of this news struck home. LaBone's gang had not yet arrived in Chama. Now Charnley had struck off on his own. Toomey had a queasy felling in the pit of his stomach that a showdown was imminent, and it was to be at the sheep farm rather than in town, as he had falsely assumed.

'Looks to me like you've seen a ghost, Sheriff,' observed Railroad Bill. 'Something sure is bugging you.'

Toomey offered no reply. Instead, he jumped to his feet, threw down a few dollar bills to pay for the meal, and left the diner in a hurry. Curious eyes followed the hasty departure of a law officer noted for his easy-going disposition. This was distinctly out of character.

He headed straight for the candy store where he knew that his deputy would be chatting up the owner. Hemp Drucker had been trying to gain the young woman's favours for some weeks without much success.

Toomey would normally have given him the benefit of his allegedly sound experience in such matters. But today was different. If his hunch was correct, big trouble was brewing.

A posse was urgently needed to ride out to stop any gunplay. But would he be in time?

When Toomey burst into the candy store, Drucker was leaning over the counter. His honeydew eyes were caressing the young girl who was purposely avoiding eye contact. The sheriff ignored the startled looks of the young couple.

'Meet me at the Alkali in ten minutes,' he ordered. 'We need to get that posse organized rapido. There's gonna be a shoot-out at the Charnley place unless we can get there fast and stop it.'

Without waiting for a reply, he hurried off down the street to gather in the men who had previously agreed to join up. Because this was an emergency he first had to get the mayor's approval to raise the participation fee to fifteen bucks a head. That wasted more time. Morgan Stanley was less than keen to spend the town funds on posse matters where a sheepherder was involved. Much to Toomey's annoyance, he prevaricated, offering weak excuses to avoid what he regarded as an unnecessary expense.

But Toomey was adamant. The peace of the whole valley was at stake here. He punched a bunched fist into the palm of his hand.

'With a gang of hardcases on the prod, far more serious trouble could flare up if'n they get away with this,' he spat out, urging the penny-pinching official to focus on the wider picture. 'They could start a range war, and might even try taking over the town.'

That was enough for the mayor. But he was insistent that the posse should consist of no more than ten men. The lawman was forced to agree.

A half-hour later, with Sheriff Toomey in the lead, they galloped out of Chama. It was going to be a race against time if a bad situation was to be averted.

11

Bushwhacked

Early sunlight heralding the onset of a new day beamed into the cave. The warming rays settled on to Rafe Charnley's haggard features, effectively rousing him from his slumber. He sat up, stretching the stiffness from his limbs.

Thankfully the storm had passed. But the water flowing down the arroyo was still waist deep. To gain the far bank, he would have to wade through it. Not an inviting prospect, but essential if he was to continue his journey.

Not wishing to delay any further he plunged into the swirling run-off which, luckily, lacked any degree of power. Thus he was able to reach the far bank without mishap. Soaked to the skin, at least he was safe. There he clambered up the slippery slope on to the level ground above. From here onwards the terrain was deeply rutted and strewn with boulders; it required extreme care to avoid injury.

To a ranch owner on the wrong side of fifty, this proved to be especially arduous. It rapidly sapped his dwindling supply of energy. His mind began to wander due to lack of food. Fatigue was also rapidly claiming his ageing frame.

Neglect of the necessary attention to the going underfoot soon took its toll. His left ankle twisted off a loosened rock.

'Aaaaagh!' A jolt of pain lanced through the wrenched joint. He couldn't prevent his tired body from keeling over. His arms flailed helplessly as he tumbled headlong down a shallow gully. As he was unable to prevent his fall, his bare head struck a boulder. And that was it. The black shadow of unconsciousness swathed the still form in its baleful embrace.

Unbeknown to the stricken man, he had reached the main east-west highway from Raton through to Chama.

Some time later, Estelle Crowther was heading towards Chama in the buggy to visit the sheriff. This would be the first time she had seen him since he returned from Wyoming. The girl was eager to catch up on his news by inviting him over to the Flying Arrow for dinner.

She would have missed the boot sticking out from behind a rock had not a curious coyote been sniffing out the potential meal. Somebody was in trouble. After chasing the scavenger off, she dismounted and hurried across to discover the comatose body of Rafe Charnley.

Apart from a cut on the head and a badly swollen ankle he appeared to be unharmed. One question loomed large in her mind. What was a lone traveller doing out here on foot and with no gear? Her initial conclusion was that he had fallen and banged his head. But that didn't explain his presence out here in the wilds.

First, however, she needed to get him to the nearest ranch. That was the sheep farm run by Jeff Charnley. She untied her bandanna, soaked it with water and dabbed the man's forehead before wiping away the blood. It had the effect of bringing some life back into the still form. Charnley groaned aloud, struggling to raise himself.

'Easy there, mister,' chided Estelle, gently pushing him back down. 'That's a nasty cut on the head. It could need stitching. And your ankle needs strapping up too.'

Charnley wasn't listening. 'I have t-to get to the r-ranch,' he stuttered out. 'My b-boy's in real d-danger.' Again he struggled to rise. This time Estelle didn't stop him. The guy's declaration had shocked her.

'Which rancher is this?' she asked.

'Jeff Charnley. He runs a sheep outfit down here.'

Estelle's eyes widened. 'You're Jeff Charnley's pa?'

He nodded. 'If'n you know where it is, take me there straight away, please.' There was more than a hint of panic in his pleading tone. The lethargic torpor induced by the bang on the head had been shrugged off. 'A gang of men are coming to kill him. And it's all down to me. They might even have arrived here before me. If'n that happens, I'll never forgive myself.'

He almost broke down in tears. But, just in time, he managed to pull himself together. It wouldn't do for a tough Wyoming rancher to display fits of emotion, especially in front of a woman.

Estelle helped him limp over to the buggy. 'It's only a mile south of here. There's a trail branching off just up ahead. We can be there in ten minutes.' She slapped the leathers, urging the horses to a steady trot.

Much as she was curious to learn about Charnley's unsettling disclosure, this was not the time to seek answers.

*　*　*

Snag LaBone and his gang had crossed the border into New Mexico around the same time as the Cumbres-Toltec

Flyer. At this point the trail branched off in three different directions. Luckily there was a sign nailed to the trunk of a pine tree. Raton to the east, south to Taos and east to Chama.

'OK, boys,' the boss declared breezily. 'East it is. We ought to be there by tomorrow noon.'

Leading the way, LaBone spurred off at a steady trot. He was eager to finish this business and make good his escape. Nobody would suspect that Wyoming killers were at the bottom of the hit. Once Charnley was given the grim facts and the ultimatum, the gang could begin raking in the dough. An avaricious gleam was reflected in his hard gaze. A half-hour later, he pulled off the main trail down a shallow draw to make camp.

The following morning, the LaBone Gang set off later than intended due the soaking they had been forced to endure during the night. Unlike Rafe Charnley, the gang had only managed to weather the storm by huddling beneath a rocky overhang, which had done little to keep them dry. It was fortunate that the next day dawned hot and sunny. Nothing saps a man's vigour and energy like wet clothes. So they all stripped off and laid their sopping duds out on the rocks.

Fishtail Emery was camp cook. Being a dab hand with a hook, line and sinker, he soon managed to catch a few trout in a nearby creek. Along with the bacon and bean tortillas, and washed down with hot coffee, the meal soon revived their flagging spirits. The gang were more than happy for the fisherman to assume the culinary role. Cooking was not on the list of their most favoured chores.

But it was not until noon before they were able to recommence the final stage of their long trek south.

Almost immediately after leaving the draw, they chanced upon a lone rider heading their way. Amos Crowther had been checking on the Questa dam to ensure that it was operating properly. He was returning to the ranch.

'Hold up there, mister.' LaBone raised a hand and pulled his horse across the trail to block off the rider's onward course.

Crowther eyed the six riders with some suspicion. They looked a tough bunch and no mistake. These guys were no regular cowhands seeking work. The twin-rigged shell belts gracing their hips spoke of gunslingers on the prod. A bead of sweat dribbled down the rancher's florid cheeks. His large moustache twitched nervously.

Affecting a degree of self-confidence that belied his churning innards, he coughed loudly before asking, 'Something I can do for you men?'

'We're looking for the Charnley spread. It's around here some place, ain't it?' replied LaBone, edging closer to the lone rider.

Crowther was taken aback by the unexpected query.

'What's your business with that guy?' he immediately blurted out. A warped sneer had replaced the quivering lip.

'You fellas sheepmen as well?'

'Listen up good, big mouth,' snarled the leader of the bunch. 'We're not here to shoot the breeze. I'm asking the questions. And if'n I don't get the right answers, it'll be the worse for you. Get my drift?' The other members of the gang had surrounded Crowther, who realized he was in no position to argue.

Had the gang known that their victim was one of the biggest ranchers in the county, they might have avoided the confrontation.

'OK, OK,' he burbled. 'No need to be so prickly. Just carry on along this road and you'll come to Apache Rock. You can't miss it. There's a rough track heading south from there that leads straight to the Charnley place. He's put up fences to mark his holding.' The rancher's face assumed an expression of disapproval.

LaBone's smile lacked any trace of mirth. 'Now that wasn't so hard was it?' The other men sniggered. 'And just so's you know, seeing as how you don't seem too keen on this guy, we have some unfinished business with Charnley that needs tidying up.'

Wiley Dobbs deliberately nudged his bay stallion into Crowther's beloved palomino, Flash, forcing the rancher to wrestle with the unnerved horse. But LaBone had found out all he wanted to know and was eager to continue the journey.

'Let's go, boys!' he ordered, swinging his horse past the skittish palomino. 'We've found out what we needed.'

But it was the crafty knife-wielder Charlie Twist who changed his mind. 'This critter looks a mite nervous,' Twist observed bluntly. 'In fact, he looks like he could cause trouble, boss. Maybe even report seeing us to the local tinstar.'

LaBone pulled up and turned to study the heavily moustached rancher, who appeared somewhat crestfallen by this unexpected turnaround. He failed miserably to conceal a guilt-laden expression. The gang leader's accusation had hit the nail on the head.

'Now that wouldn't be very advisable, would it, boys?' the boss intoned in his usual ironic manner.

A restless murmuring of irritation rippled through the ranks of the bunching riders. LaBone's easy-going detachment continued but it was laced with a chilling menace as he cast a threatening glower at the hovering rancher. 'You're coming with us, fella, to show us the way. Make sure we don't get lost. At least until our . . . erm . . . business is concluded. Then, if'n you've been a good boy, maybe I'll consider letting you go.'

'I won't say a word,' Crowther protested vigorously, trying desperately to swim against a lethal current. 'I ain't bothered what happens to Charnley. Anybody that runs sheep in this country is no friend of mine.'

It was a futile endeavour. LaBone's mind was made up. He was taking no unnecessary risks. 'Grab his shooter, Wildcat.'

Crowther was quickly disarmed and

his hands tied. With the woebegone ranch owner held between them, the gang then moved off, heading for their terminal rendezvous with Jeff Charnley.

* * *

When Estelle and her forlorn passenger reached the sheepherder's small cabin she drew the buggy to a halt. Experience had taught her that it was a foolish person who rode straight into any lonely outpost without first announcing their presence.

She was aware of too many innocent visitors who had been gunned down by nervous settlers.

'Hallo, the cabin,' she called out. 'Anybody home?'

Apart from the chirping of a cactus wren perched on the roof, there was no answer.

Rafe Charnley heaved his tired body off the buggy and limped over to the cabin. 'You in there, Jeff?' he hollered, his voice cracked and raw. 'It's your pa.

I want you to come home, son. I've been a danged fool.'

Still no response. There was no smoke dribbling from the stovepipe, a further indication that the place was unoccupied.

'Don't look like there's anybody home, Mr Charnley,' said Estelle, nudging the buggy round the side of the line structure. 'You stay here while I take a look around. He could be out back someplace.'

Five minutes later she was back. 'Maybe he's gone into Chama for supplies,' she said. It was the only thing that either of them could think of. Charnley walked across to the door and pushed it open. Estelle joined him. The cabin was rather untidy but no more so than any regular bunkhouse. At least it was clean. Jeff had obviously learned something from his time at the Flying Arrow. Orderliness with everything in its place equates to efficiency and a successful enterprise. That was a quotation often reeled out by Rafe

Charnley to his men.

'I reckon we ought to hang around here for a spell,' the girl recommended. 'If'n he don't turn up within an hour, then we can head for town. Could be we'll meet him on the way back.'

Charnley was decidedly twitchy. Worry lines creased his face. 'LaBone and his rats could already have snatched the boy,' he croaked, wringing his hands. 'Maybe I'm too late.'

'We don't know that,' Estelle offered, attempting to ease the tension. 'There's nobody here now. Nothing appears to have been broken, which would point to an attack.'

'Guess I am being a bit unreasonable.'

'You have every right to be,' the girl agreed. 'If what you say is the case, Jeff's life is in grave danger.'

Estelle lit a fire in the grate and set a pot of water on to boil. 'A strong mug of coffee will help pass the time.'

She had also found a slab of bacon and some potatoes in a sack. Knowing that Charnley had not eaten for a couple of days, she soon had the skillet sizzling.

The rancher slumped into a home-made armchair that was more comfortable than it looked. Estelle had strapped up his ankle, which helped to ease the pain. The older man was unquestionably weary following his austere trek from Pagosa Springs. But the delicious aroma of frying bacon made his mouth water. In the interim he made do by dipping into a tin of cookies.

That was all he was destined to eat.

Snag LaBone had just arrived at the homestead and would shortly make his presence known in a brutally stark manner.

'There's somebody at home,' announced Bulldog Lannigan, pointing to the twirl of smoke drifting skywards from the chimney. 'You figure it's Charnley, boss?'

'Don't reckon it can be anyone else,' replied LaBone. 'This is his place. That's right, ain't it, mister?' he said to Amos Crowther.

The rancher concurred. 'He lives alone. There's supposed to be a sweetheart on her way down here to join him. But she ain't turned up yet.' Crowther locked a pleading eye on to the gang boss. 'I've done what you asked and led you here. So when you gonna let me go?'

In truth, LaBone had no intention of freeing the captive. He knew that the guy's first move would be to alert the authorities to their ambush. But he intended playing along until the job had been completed.

'Not until I'm satisfied that Charnley is a goner.' His next order was to Charlie Twist. 'Make sure this guy don't cause us no problems during the shindig.'

Twist aimed a humourless smile at the quaking rancher. 'This way, hot shot. And one word of warning to yon sheep-dipper, and I'll tickle your ribs with this fella.' He drew the lethal ten-inch Bowie knife from his belt. Crowther's eyes bulged, his face turning a dull shade of grey.

'OK, boys, it's party time,' LaBone hissed. He ordered his men to surround the cabin. 'Check your guns are fully loaded. And make sure every window is covered. It's only a one-roomed shack. He won't stand a chance once we open up. But nobody cuts loose until I've fired the first shot. Then let the skunk have it with everything you've got.'

LaBone crept as close to the front of the cabin as possible without exposing himself. A water trough offered the ideal place, opposite the door. He held his fire until a shadow was seen passing across the main window.

Inside the cabin, Rafe had noticed the makings for a smoke on the fireplace. He stood up and hobbled across.

That was when all hell broke loose. He didn't stand a chance. A bullet struck him in the chest. He staggered, gripping the table.

'Got him!' yelled the exultant voice of Snag LaBone. A seething bloodlust had infected the owlhooter's whole being.

Demented eyes blazed with an insatiable hunger to kill. 'Keep it up, boys. Like as not he's only wounded. We can't take any chances of the varmint walking away from this.'

The gunfire resumed with increased ferocity.

Estelle was lucky that when the shooting started she was bent over the skillet. Hot lead flew all around her as the glass in the three windows shattered into a million sharp fragments. The noise was deafening as the deadly barrage continued without interruption for what seemed like a dozen lifetimes.

She threw herself down on the earthen floor as bullets zipped and whined in all directions. A few shards of glass nicked her skin, but she barely felt them — such was her fear. She hugged the floor. Both hands clutched her head trying to shut out the awful racket.

In fact the gunfire lasted for little more than one minute. Only when all the gun loads had been expended did the deadly onslaught cease. The silence that followed was almost palpable, although the ringing in her ears continued like a clanging church bell.

Only then did she notice the still form lying at an unnatural angle beside the fireplace. A gasp of shock and disbelief clouded her ashen features. Even from where she was cowering, she could see three bullet wounds. Assuming that Rafe Charnley was dead, the terrified girl's main concern now was to escape. She could hear the leader of the assailants cheering maniacally.

Then a far more sinister directive reached her ears.

'Let's give this dude a funeral his pa would be proud of.'

'What's on your mind, boss?' gurgled the demented snicker of Wiley Dobbs.

'We'll burn the place down.' A laugh charged with frantic intensity infected his followers, who joined in the demonic euphoria.

'Yeeeehaaaaa!' cackled diminutive Charlie Twist. 'That's a great idea, boss.'

So concentrated were the gang on

revelling in their victorious assault, they forgot about Amos Crowther. Although the rancher was impeded by his bonds, he managed to crawl away from the riotous gathering. That was when he saw a slender figure climb out of the shack's shattered rear window. His eyes widened in shock on recognizing the profile of Estelle.

So taken aback was he by the presence of his beloved sister that Crowther could not contain a cry of surprise.

'Estelle!' he called out. 'What are you doing here? Get away quickly while you can.' Too late he realized his error.

LaBone's alerted ears heard the panic-filled exclamation. He hurried across to see what was happening. That was when he saw the girl trying to flee from the scene of devastation. A growl erupted from his twisted maw.

'Much obliged for the warning, fella,' he snarled. 'A pity it won't do you any good.' Without any further ado he hauled off his final bullet.

Crowther didn't stand a chance.

Estelle was stunned into immobility by the sudden downing of her brother. All she could do was stand there like a statue as the killer advanced towards her. A lascivious licking of his thin lips was enough to impart what the murderous gangleader had in mind.

But all was not lost.

12

Too Late?

When he heard the gunfire on the far side of a low range of hills, Sheriff Toomey urged his men forward. It had to be the LaBone gang, who were intent on punching home the final nail in their intended victim's coffin. Cresting the ridge, he could see that his supposition had been correct.

Below, the fierce gun battle had just finished. A quick scan of the blood-curdling scene told him that the fight was all one-sided. Was he too late to save the occupant of the cabin?

Praying that this was not the case, the sheriff drew his revolver and let fly with a couple of shots to distract the attackers. His bullets were wide of the mark, but at least he had drawn attention away from anybody cowering inside the cabin.

'Take cover, men,' he called out urgently. 'And make every bullet count.' The possemen leapt off their horses and scattered among the rocks.

The smugly satisfied leer cloaking the face of Snag LaBone was instantly removed on his discovering they were not alone.

'Looks like we've got company, boss.' The worried observation from Bulldog Lannigan made the others look to their rear. 'What now?'

'What d'yuh damned well think?' the outlaw leader snapped out in reply. 'Let the bastards have it.'

But the trouble was their guns were empty following the deadly attack on the cabin. Panic-stricken hands feverishly struggled to reload. This gave the new attackers the chance to pick them off without encountering any return fire.

The first to go down under the fusillade of shots was Dick Shifter. A look of terror spread across the leathery features of Fishtail Emery who now found himself crouching beside the dead man. Though his revolver was empty the outlaw made a spirited dash across to his horse. He dragged out a Henry repeater and managed to loose off a couple of shots before he himself was forced to chew on a lethal dose of hot lead.

The posse members cheered ecstatically as two of the outlaws were quickly removed from the affray. The tables appeared to have been quickly turned. But Snag LaBone was no pushover. He urged his men to fight back.

'These dupes are town hicks,' he called out. 'They ain't used to dealing with tough guys like us. So let's show them who's calling the shots around here.'

In his excitement one of the Chama men foolishly jumped into the air, unwittingly exposing his too corpulent frame. This enabled Charlie Twist to effectively demonstrate his deadly knife-throwing talent. Chet Stirling only realized the magnitude of his greenhorn blunder when the deadly blade skewered him in the chest. No more beers would be pulled by the Alkali saloon's jovial bartender.

Seeing one of their buddies bite the dust had a chastening effect on the rest of the posse. Death had come a-calling. They were indeed a mixture of store clerks and office dudes. Gunfighting was not their usual sphere of activity. Suddenly, this caper was no longer an exciting adventure, but a deadly tussle where the grim reaper held all the best cards.

But the posse still held the higher ground. The outlaws were outgunned and were still reloading their pistols. Toomey saw that his men were wilting after the brutal slaying of the popular barman. Anxious to maintain the upper hand, he quickly exhorted them to take advantage of their opponents' weakened state by moving forward in a pincer movement to hem them in.

Wiley Dobbs was a recent addition to

LaBone's gang. This job was turning out to be far more dangerous than he had expected. The easy pickings promised by LaBone were now a distant memory. He wanted out.

The demoralized outlaw tried to make a dash for his horse to escape across the open ground. But he stood no chance as half a dozen slugs peppered his body. Revitalized, the posse did as instructed by their leader, making sure to keep their heads down.

LaBone scowled as his nervous eye lit upon the tin star of the posse leader. His dirt-smeared face was leaking nervous sweat. He recognized Toomey from the brief sighting in Casper. It was now clear that the writing was on the wall and that the message boded ill for his survival. The fight was going against them.

Yet, ever the resourceful schemer, he was now looking out for his own survival. The answer was right beside him.

Estelle was so distraught by what had taken place that her brain had ceased to function. She was in a virtual state of limbo. Hugging the ground as the rattle of gunfire continued all around, her slim body trembled with terror. The shooting of Rafe Charnley followed by that of her own brother was more than any person could handle.

'You're coming with me, girl,' LaBone snapped, roughly hauling her up. 'I'm getting out of here and you're gonna be my insurance policy.'

Any thought for the rest of his crew had been abandoned. It was now every man for himself. In the back of his unhinged brain was the nagging quandary of how these guys had known what was happening. He had no idea that Heck Toomey had been spying on him and had learned the grim truth. He slung an arm roughly around the girl's neck.

The first intimation Heck Toomey had that his lady love was involved in the fracas was a loud gut-churning scream of terror. Her brutal man-handling by the fleeing gang boss had jerked the distraught girl's mind to a full realization of the horror of her predicament.

The frightful howl wrenched from her throat was barely human in its feverish vehemence. It was a cry of pure desperation to attract the attention of her sweetheart. LaBone reacted with a snarl of rage which was accompanied by a solid backhander. The jarring blow effectively curtailed the girl's outburst. Blood dribbled from a split lip as she fell to the ground.

But the wretched cry for help had not passed unnoticed. Toomey's searching gaze homed in on the struggling female and her brutal assailant. He sucked in a desperate gulp of air. Shock at seeing the woman he loved in the hands of the hard-boiled killer brought a lump to his throat.

Much to his chagrin, Toomey knew that he was stymied. LaBone snatched up the girl and jammed a gun into her swanlike neck.

'Come any closer and the dame gets

it,' he shouted. 'Now tell your boys to back off.' He jabbed his gun menacingly. The lawman had no doubt that the rat would haul off at the slightest provocation.

'You heard him,' Toomey ordered his men. 'Cease fire. He's got Miss Crowther down there.' The reason for her presence never entered the lawman's head. He knew only that she was in grave danger.

A tense lull in the battle followed. It was a stalemate.

LaBone had no intention of lingering. Using the girl as a shield he dragged her back behind the cabin over to where the buggy had been left. It was not the best means of transport for a cross-country flight, but it would have to suffice. For now.

'Move it, sister!' he barked in her ear. 'And remember. The slightest attempt to escape and there's a bullet here with your name on it.'

Estelle was terrified, but she had no choice. She must comply.

'What about us, boss?' came the plaintive appeal from Wildcat Mancos. 'These critters have gotten us pinned down over here.'

LaBone was not listening. His hide was on the line and that was all that mattered to the cowardly owlhoot. Once he had the girl seated in the buggy he whipped up the horse, urging the animal off in the opposite direction from where the gunfight had been taking place.

Initially his flight was obscured by the cabin. Only when a plume of dust twined up behind it did Toomey realize what the outlaw had in mind.

LaBone intended holding Estelle as a hostage until such time as she had served her purpose. He knew that the sheriff would not want any harm to befall her. That was the way of the West. Apart from soiled doves and saloon gals, women were held in high regard. Any regular guy worth his salt would not purposely place them in jeopardy.

The abductor knew that and he

intended taking full advantage of the chivalric code of honour. He figured rightly that all Toomey could do was follow at a distance and pray for some opportunity to thwart the skunk's odious scheme.

The killer intended to be over the border and into the lawless panhandle territory of no man's land before Toomey caught up.

Following him into that devil's lair would be like sticking his head in a hornets' nest.

Wildcat Mancos quickly realized that the game was up when the surviving members of the gang were left in the lurch. There were only three of them left to take on the larger force, and they were pinned down with no place to go. Even knowing the posse were only regular townsmen did not shift the odds in their favour.

It was time to cut their losses and plead ignorance. Any charges would have to be laid at LaBone's door. After all, it could be claimed that he was the one who had fired the fatal shots. The yellow rat deserved nothing less. It would mean a jail term. But that was better than the alternative.

'LaBone's left us to take all the blame, boys,' Mancos hollered across to his two remaining buddies. 'He's lit out with the girl in that buggy.'

'What we gonna do, Wildcat?' asked the tremulous Lannigan. All his bulldog tenacity had drained away. The guy was a follower, not a leader.

'Time to call it quits, and take our chances with the law,' Mancos replied. 'It's better than staying here to be picked off one by one. What do you say, Charlie?'

'It was all LaBone's doing anyway,' grunted the morose knife-wielder. 'Let him carry the can. I'm with you, Wildcat.'

The tough hardcase raised his voice. 'You listening, Sheriff?' he hollered.

'I'm here, fella.' The blunt reply floated across the bleak killing ground. 'What is it you have to say?'

'If'n you promise to speak up for us at a trial, we'll surrender now without any further bloodshed. All this was LaBone's plan anyway. And it was him that killed Charnley.' Mancos waited a moment for the import of his words to sink in. 'So what do you say, Sheriff? Is it a deal?'

'I don't cut any deals with outlaws,' Toomey snapped back. 'But if'n you give up now, I'll make sure that the court knows about it.'

That was all the downcast outlaws could hope for. Mancos threw his guns out into the open. He was followed moments later by the others.

'Keep your hands high and no funny business,' rapped the lawman. He was anxious to set off on the trail of the fleeing gang boss. But an innate caution prevented any rash move on his part. Too often in the past he had seen less experienced lawman cut down by trickery. Consequently, he remained stationed behind a rock as two of the gang emerged from cover.

Two of the posse immediately showed themselves. Grins wider than the Rio Grande were spread across their faces. They had stood up against a gang of hardbitten roughnecks and come out on top. This was going to be a topic of conversation and prestige for weeks to come.

As Mancos and Bulldog Lannigan showed themselves, hands reaching skywards, Charlie Twist had other ideas. No way was he spending the next few years in the territorial pen. Guns blazing, he cut down one of the naive posse men as he hurried across to mount up. The guy clutched his chest and fell to the ground, an inane grin still pasted on to his callow features.

The other man immediately recognized the danger he had so innocently dismissed and fell to the ground. His nerves were shaken to the core as his staring eyes beheld his friend's life blood leaking out of the punctured torso.

The response to Charlie Twist's unexpected defiance was delayed as men's addled brains strove to interpret the sudden upset.

Twist took full advantage of the lull by sprinting across to his horse and leaping into the saddle. That was when the bubble burst. Badly aimed slugs buzzed round his head, none of which found their mark.

A small guy, Twist kept his head down, swinging away to make good his escape. It was the calm deliberation of Heck Toomey that eventually brought the attempted flight to an inglorious finale. The sheriff levered a fresh round into the barrel of his Winchester, took careful aim and let fly.

The first bullet plucked Twist's hat from his lowered head. But the second saw his hands windmilling helplessly as the lethal charge bit deep into his back. Like a discarded rag doll, he was flung out of the saddle into the spike-loaded embrace of a thorn bush.

The carbine swung to cover the other two startled outlaws. 'Try anything like that and there won't be no trial,'

Toomey rasped, peering acidly down the barrel of the long gun. 'Just a double plot on Boot Hill.'

13

Silver Tongue

Once the two dejected crooks had been securely bound and were no longer a threat, Toomey wanted to get after LaBone.

'You're in charge, Hemp. Make sure these critters are locked up tight as a whalebone corset when you get 'em back to town,' the sheriff instructed his deputy. 'I'm going after Miss Crowther.'

'Do you need any help, Sheriff?' asked a thoroughly chastened Zeke Chadwick, who had nearly had his head blown off moments before. The store-keeper desperately wanted to atone for the embarrassing blunder that had almost cost him his life.

'I sure do, Zeke,' replied the lawman, 'but the skill I require ain't concerned with selling dry goods.' His pointed gaze fell upon Kingpin Muldoon. 'I need a guy with the gift of the gab. A good talker. A fella that could mouth his way into Clinton's Bank and come out with an interest-free loan.'

Toomey had a feeling that delicate negotiation was going to play a big part in his effort to rescue Estelle Crowther. Muldoon was going to be his mouth-piece.

'You up for this, Kingpin?' the lawman intoned hopefully. 'Your mouth and my guns should make for a solid team. So what d'you say?'

The rodeo master of ceremonies was delighted to have been accorded the confidence of the lawman. 'I'd be proud to help out, Sheriff,' he answered, adding a proviso: 'Just so long as you ain't expecting a sharp-shooter as well as a gab man.'

'Don't worry. Any gunplay will be between me and that yellow-belly of a hostage-taker.'

Without further ado, the two pursu-ers set off in the direction taken by the buggy.

Two hours passed with no sign of the fleeing outlaw and his captive. But Toomey was not worried. The ruts left by the buggy were clearly etched into the sandy ground. The sheriff and his associate had reached the bottom end of the valley when, cresting a low rise, a startling sight was revealed. The lawman drew to a halt behind some boulders.

Below, in a shallow amphitheatre, stood a lone cottonwood tree in the middle of the open tract. Securely pinioned to the trunk was Estelle Crowther. The abandoned buggy was close by, the horse grazing contentedly on some grass.

The girl was dishevelled and looked to have been roughly treated by her captor. Her head drooped to one side. Toomey held his breath. The awful notion struck him that she might be dead. Tears welled up in his eyes. Then her head moved, only slightly, but enough to assure the watchers that she was still in the land of the living. A whoosh of air hissed from between the sheriff's clenched jaws as he breathed again. His relief was tempered by a seething hunger to avenge her suffering.

His hate-filled eyes panned the terrain. Of the abductor there was no sign, although he had to be close at hand, and was clearly awaiting the lawman's arrival.

'What do you reckon he's up to, Sheriff?' inquired a mystified Muldoon.

Toomey was also baffled. Some skulduggery was afoot. 'The rat has obviously arrived at the conclusion that a buggy is no use as an escape vehicle in this country. But I have no idea which way his warped mind is shifting. The only way to find out what game the skunk is playing is to ask him.'

Muldoon's grizzled visage registered even more confusion at this suggestion.

Toomey thought hard for a few minutes, striving to formulate a plan that would work. The key lay in persuading the abductor that he, Toomey, was alone.

Having tossed around a few ideas in his head, he then explained his proposed scheme to Muldoon. The essence of its success lay in the chat man assuming the role of sheriff.

'Give me about ten minutes to get behind those rocks over yonder. Then call out what we agreed. Savvy?'

Muldoon nodded, eager to play his part in the bizarre drama that was about to unfold.

'After that it'll be your silvery tongue that will have to hold the jasper's attention until I'm ready to make my play.' The sheriff then slipped silently away.

Minutes ticked by. At the appointed time Kingpin Muldoon sucked in a deep breath and called out:

'This is Sheriff Heck Toomey speaking. I'm here to rescue Miss Crowther and arrest you for murder. The game's up, mister. Best thing for you now is to come out with your hands high. You'll never be able to get that buggy through the mountains.'

Muldoon sounded nothing like Heck Toomey, but that was of no consequence. The outlaw had never heard the sheriff's distinctive voice.

This sudden declaration brought a stirring from the captive, whose head slowly lifted. A startled expression on her face replaced one of utter helplessness. The strident announcement that she heard drifting across the open sward momentarily threw her into a quandary. That certainly was not the gravelly tones of her beloved. But she remained tight-lipped, rightly assuming that it was some kind of subterfuge to trick her abductor. A gleam of renewed hope lit up her face.

A jovial chortle echoed around the rock-girt arena. It originated from a grove of trees some way to the left of where Toomey was secreted.

'Good try, tinstar. But what you're forgetting is that I'm holding all the aces.'

Toomey smiled. LaBone had fallen for the stratagem hook, line and sinker.

'And there's a rifle trained on the dame. One false move from you and she gets it.'

Estelle quaked in terror. Muldoon

shivered. This guy clearly had no intention of surrendering. However, the gab man continued the dialogue so as to maintain the deception.

'What do you have in mind?' he called. 'With you over there, me over here, and the girl in the middle it looks like a no-win situation to me.'

'That's cos you ain't got the brain of Snag LaBone. Ha-ha-ha!'

The uproarious cackling grated on Muldoon's nerves. He felt the urge to haul off with his rifle at the taunting sneer. But that would ruin everything. Exerting the greatest effort, he held his nerve as he shouted back:

'So what's the play?'

'I need a fast horse. Send your cayuse out into the open and make sure all your hardware is draped over the saddle horn. Remember: try pulling any crazy stunts and the girl is dead meat. Now get to it, pronto!'

Moments later Muldoon slapped his horse on the rump, urging the animal into view. As expected, it trotted over to join the grazing buggy mare. As directed, Muldoon's gunbelt and rifle were in full view.

'Smart move, Sheriff,' intoned the outlaw, emerging from his place of concealment. He was clutching a rifle. 'Now show yourself so that I know where you are.'

'H-how do I know you w-won't drill me?' stuttered the decidedly nervous Kingpin.

'No need for that now your teeth have been pulled,' breezed an upbeat LaBone. 'I just want to have one last glimpse of the tough sheriff with egg splattered all over his ugly mug. Seeing you helpless as a baby will keep my spirits up all the way to the panhandle.'

Another peal of bitter laughter rang out as Muldoon gingerly emerged from cover. He was wearing the sheriff's trademark grey hat and black leather vest with the shiny star glinting in the sun.

'That's far enough,' LaBone rapped out.

Keeping a wary eye on the sham lawman, the braggart moved across to the horse. He was about to mount up when another voice rang out immediately behind him.

'That's far enough, ratface,' the sheriff growled. 'Now it's my turn to take the reins.' The killer was taken completely by surprise. His leathery face registered shocked bewilderment. But it was only a momentary pause.

'Don't try it, scumbag. There's a bullet here with your name on it.' The ominous click of a rifle being levered effectively supported Toomey's blunt threat. Quick as lightning he hurried across to where the outlaw was pondering his chances. 'Now turn around slow and easy,' the lawman ordered.

LaBone knew that he had been suckered, that he had little option now but to comply. Face to face, all Toomey's anger burst forth as he put his whole weight behind his forward-lunging right arm. His tightly bunched fist smashed into the outlaw's face. It was a solid punch that jerked the guy off his feet.

A glazed look in the lawman's eyes boded ill for the recipient of his anger. Reaching down, he dragged the stunned LaBone to his feet and planted another solid jab right on the button. LaBone screamed as his mashed nose exploded. The irate sheriff was all set to deliver more of the same. Only the restraining hand of Kingpin Muldoon prevented the enraged lawman from upending all that for which he stood.

'The skunk ain't worth it, Sheriff,' Muldoon pressed. 'He's finished. So let the courts do their job in the manner prescribed by the law you are paid to uphold.'

'He's right, honey.' Estelle had finally found her voice. 'Vigilante justice has no place in your book. Heck Toomey is above all that.'

The woman's dulcet tones effectively lifted the dark veil of revulsion that had threatened to consume the upright and principled lawman.

'You're right,' he muttered, some-what chastened by his uncharacteristic loss of control. 'It was seeing you all trussed up that made me lose the thread.'

He shook off the unnatural malaise, quickly reverting back to his regular level-headed dependability.

'Tie this piece of horse dung up tighter than a Thanksgiving turkey and get him on to his horse,' he ordered Muldoon as he freed the relieved victim of her bonds.

The two lovers fell into each other's arms. He tenderly stroked her hair. 'I'd never have forgiven myself if any harm had come to you,' murmured the relieved lawman into her ear. They kissed. It was the first time. Realizing that they were being observed by the grinning Muldoon, the happy pair quickly parted.

'OK, let's ride,' Toomey ordered to hide his bashful coyness. He helped Estelle up on to the seat of the buggy, then went and retrieved his own mount.

* * *

When the rescue party and their prisoner reached Chama they were met by the other members of the posse. LaBone was left in their capable if somewhat robust hands. This skunk was responsible for gunning down their friends. The sheriff harboured no sympathy and studiously ignored the killer's plea for sanctuary when he was dragged off his horse.

He and Estelle went inside the jailhouse to be met by Deputy Hemp Drucker. 'You were right about the elder Charnley being at the cabin,' he said. Toomey nodded. He had already been apprised of this by Estelle.

'Was he . . . ?' The sheriff gulped, unable to complete the inquiry.

All the way back to town he had convinced himself that the rancher must have died in the furious gun battle. His hackles rose as the lethal demons of retribution once again threatened to overwhelm him. Only the steadying influence of Estelle and Kingpin Muldoon prevented him from embarking on a deadly course of action against the killer, from which there would be no way back.

'That guy is like the cat with nine lives,' declared the deputy. 'And he used up eight of them in that cabin. But he's still here to tell the tale.' A flush of relief washed over Toomey's face. 'He's hurt bad,' the deputy continued. 'We took him over to Doc Spoonbill's surgery soon as we got back here. He's over there now. It was touch and go whether he would pull through the night. But the doc is confident that he'll make a full recovery.'

'That's good news,' said Estelle. 'But the mystery still remains about what has happened to Jeff Charnley. Have you seen him?' she asked of the hovering deputy.

Drucker's raised eyebrow shifted towards his boss.

Toomey did not say anything. Instead he called out, 'You up there, boy?'

Moments later the figure of none other than Jeff Charnley came down the stairs from the living quarters he had been sharing with the lawman. Meanwhile Toomey had decided that LaBone himself needed rescuing from the irate chastisement that was being administered outside.

'OK, boys, that's enough of the rough stuff,' he ordered. 'Bring him inside.'

Seeing the object of his heinous scheme standing there was a shock to the system for Snag LaBone. He couldn't believe what his peepers were telling him.

'You!' he exclaimed. 'It can't be. We gunned you down in the cabin.'

'You would have done if'n the sheriff here hadn't warned me of your lowdown plan.' Jeff's face twisted in anger as he lunged at the manacled prisoner. Only the forceful intervention of Hemp Drucker prevented more disfigurement to the bruised features of the outlaw. LaBone was hustled away to the cell block to join the surviving members of his gang.

'Best put the varmint in a separate cell, Hemp,' Toomey advised the young deputy. 'I need him to be still alive come trial day.' Then he turned back to Jeff Charnley and explained all that had happened. 'The varmint's game backfired on him all right. And he's gonna face a court of law along with his cronies for this.'

He had persuaded Jeff that it was in everyone's interests that he return to Chama to ensure his safety. 'I knew this bunch of killers were gunning for Jeff. But I didn't know where they planned to make the hit. That's why I brought him here,' he explained to the bewildered Estelle. 'I couldn't take any unnecessary risks.'

Young Charnley's brow furrowed in puzzlement. 'If'n it wasn't me in that cabin when those rats attacked, then who stopped lead on my account?'

14

Reconciliation

Toomey gulped. 'It was your father, son. He came out here to warn you that LaBone was on his way down from Wyoming.'

Then it struck the young man what had really happened 'This is all my father's doing, isn't it? He sent these men to get me. How could he do that to his only son?' A further wave of bitterness assailed the young hot-head. He had completely forgotten the fact that someone else had been shot down in his place. 'Sure we've had our differences,' he ranted on, oblivious of his father's dire situation, 'and I've made him pay for his stubborn attitude towards me. But sending killers to wipe me out . . . ?'

'Hold up there, kid,' Toomey's sharp

retort abruptly cut off the angry tirade. 'It was your father that took the lead meant for you, remember. That's why he came down here. To stop LaBone carrying out his orders. Now he's fighting for his life, and all you can do is cast blame elsewhere. Both of you two mule heads are responsible for all this trouble.' An accusatory finger jabbed the boy in the chest as Toomey was all set to deliver more furious remarks.

Estelle now stepped forward to relieve the growing tension.

'This is no time for throwing stones at each other,' she declared softly but with a firm resolve. Turning to address Jeff, she said, 'Don't you think the time has come to show some compassion, some forgiveness? Hold your hand out in peace? Your father might have died in that cabin. I was there. Knowing what has happened, I'm certain that he is anxious to bury the past and start anew.'

Young Charnley's twisted features suggested that he was set to toss the olive branch aside. Then, the significance of the girl's blunt remarks struck home. All the anger and resentment that had built up over the last few months was suddenly released. It was as if the sun had come out from behind a dark cloud.

His head fell on to his chest at the realization of all that had taken place: all that anger and frustration, the need to hit back, humiliate his father. For what? Now he was lying in a hospital bed, his life in the balance. All because his wayward son had chosen the path of revenge.

Heck Toomey saw that young Jeff Charnley was now full of remorse. He also knew that the desperately ill man was equally at fault. Both father and son had exhibited a degree of hard-headed obstinacy that could quite easily have rampaged out of control.

'It wasn't all your doing, Jeff,' he placated the distraught boy. 'Your pa has just as much need of forgiveness in many ways. I'm just glad that both of you have seen the light before it was too late.'

Without further ado, Jeff left the jail and headed down town for the surgery.

Standing at the bedside of his father, Jeff Charnley's eyes filled with tears as he listened intently while the injured man poured out all the sordid details of his plan to teach the boy a lesson. Plans that had so catastrophically backfired.

Once again, Jeff felt the anger rising inside him.

'How could you have set those rats on me, Pa,' he said accusingly. 'You knew what sort of lowlife Snag LaBone was.'

'I wasn't thinking straight,' admitted Charnley. 'All I wanted was to scare you into coming back to Wyoming so we could work together. The last thing I wanted was for any harm to befall you. I swear on your mother's life, that's the truth.'

Jeff saw the misery over what had occurred in his father's distressed expression. His own resentment wilted accordingly. Then he recalled the words of Estelle Crowther about the act of forgiveness.

He held out a hand. His father grasped it firmly, watery eyes lighting up.

'Guess we've both acted like stubborn fools.' Jeff's lowered voice was full of contrition. 'Neither of us could see the harm we were setting in motion. Surely it ain't too late to turn the clock back and start again. That's all I want now.'

'No need for that, Jeff,' replied his jubilant father. 'We can go forward and make certain we have learned a valuable lesson from our mistakes. When I saw that I'd almost gotten you killed, I knew that my craving for power and prestige had overshadowed everything that was truly worthwhile. Come back to the ranch and we'll run it together. And this time, I'll listen up and take heed of other people's viewpoints.'

Their handshake was firm and cemented by a new understanding that family loyalty and kinship is more important than any display of authority and influence.

It was another two weeks before Rafe Charnley was sufficiently recovered from his injuries to leave the hospital. In the meantime, Jeff had sold his holding to Amos Crowther, and the sheep to a buyer from Santa Fe.

The two Wyoming men were at the railroad depot, about to board the train back home. They had been joined by Heck Toomey and his new fiancée.

Her brother Amos was also there. Although the feisty rancher was more eager to witness the back of the pair the reconciliation was welcome. Even more so was the departure of the sheep. The Feather Bend rancher would not be able to settle until they were well and truly out of his hair.

Amos had plans for the land he had just bought and woollies had no place in them.

The conductor blew his whistle. 'All aboard, folks,' he called out. 'First stop

Pagosa Springs to take on water.' Rafe shivered at mention of the ominous halt, as he recalled his last visit. 'All being well, we should be at Antonio by nightfall.'

The three men shook hands. Estelle planted a brief peck on Jeff's cheek. 'You make sure to let us know how things go up there,' she told him. 'And remember what can happen when families break down.'

'We ain't about to make that mistake again, you can be sure of that, Miss Crowther,' Rafe assured the girl as he climbed aboard the train.

Soon after, the lonesome whistle blew and the Cumbres-Toltec Flyer pulled out of Chama.

'Can't say that I'm sorry to see them go,' intoned the jaundiced voice of Amos Crowther. He ignored the sour regard from his sister. 'This fracas almost started a range war. And it's thanks to you, Heck, that everything turned out fine.'

'I'm more relieved that a blood feud was avoided and that a father and son have been reunited,' said the sheriff.

'And I second that,' agreed Estelle, slipping a hand through his arm.

* * *

Thankfully there were no delays on the return journey to Casper. As the train pulled into the station, Rafe nudged his son in the ribs.

'Take a look out there, son. Isn't it a sight for sore eyes?'

Jeff offered his father a quizzical frown. But he looked in the direction of the pointing hand. That was when his face registered shocked surprise, but it was a decidedly pleasant feeling that spread its warmth throughout his body. There on the platform was none other than Elsa Fallenborg.

'Cat gotten your tongue, boy?' His father's broad grin spread from ear to ear.

'B-but, I don't u-understand . . . ' stammered the younger Charnley.

Rafe was more than happy to explain.

'I wired her two days ago to meet us here. According to Curly Bob, the gal has been pestering him about what has happened to you. I figured it was only right to let her know the outcome.' He paused to allow Jeff's addled brain to catch up. 'I also told her father that I'd sell him some land at a knockdown price. There's more than enough room for sheep and cattle to exist side by side in the Big Horn.'

Jeff was not listening. All his attention was directed towards the girl of his dreams. He hurried off the train on to the platform, where the two young lovers fell into each other's arms.

A Wyoming blood feud had been averted and a new era of cooperation had been fostered. And it was all down to a certain New Mexico lawman and his betrothed.

We do hope that you have enjoyed reading this large print book.

Did you know that all of our titles are available for purchase?

We publish a wide range of high quality large print books including:
Romances, Mysteries, Classics
General Fiction
Non Fiction and Westerns

Special interest titles available in large print are:
The Little Oxford Dictionary
Music Book, Song Book
Hymn Book, Service Book

Also available from us courtesy of Oxford University Press:
Young Readers' Dictionary
(large print edition)
Young Readers' Thesaurus
(large print edition)

For further information or a free brochure, please contact us at:
Ulverscroft Large Print Books Ltd.,
The Green, Bradgate Road, Anstey,
Leicester, LE7 7FU, England.
Tel: (00 44) **0116 236 4325**
Fax: (00 44) **0116 234 0205**

Other titles in the
Linford Western Library:

THE LAW IN CROSSROADS

J. L. Guin

Jack Bonner, former lawman, has retired to the small town of Crossroads, Texas. But when a rogue gunman shoots up a saloon, Bonner feels obligated to investigate, as there is no lawman in town. He reluctantly agrees to take on temporary marshal duties. Things go sour when Z Bar ranch owner Horace Davies hires a known gunman instead of cowboys, turning the Z Bar into a haven for outlaws. And when Davies offers a reward for Bonner's demise, Jack goes into action . . .

ALL MUST DIE

I. J. Parnham

Ten years ago, a spree of murders shocked the townsfolk of Monotony. The victims were shot and dumped, with words scrawled on the ground beside them. When Sykes Caine was arrested for a bank raid, the killings stopped . . . Now Sheriff Cassidy Yates must deal with a perplexing case. A man is shot to death — and words are scratched into the ground by the corpse. With Sykes now released from jail and back in town, the finger of suspicion is pointed squarely at him . . .

LONELY IS THE GUNFIGHTER

Steve Hayes

Morgan 'Coop' Cooper is a man with a tragic past and an uncertain future. Drifting into the town of Rocas Rojas, his trail crosses with that of enigmatic saloon owner Lorna Rutledge. They hit it off immediately — but there is more to Lorna than meets the eye. Almost before he knows it, Coop finds himself teamed up with a gunman named Gospel Curtis, and robbing a gold train at Deep River Gorge . . .

THE WIDELOOPERS

Corba Sunman

Tod Bailey rides out of Dodge City a happy man. He has sold his herd, and the only job remaining before collecting his payment is to deliver the beef to the buyer's corrals. But his cheerful mood will not last long. Upon his arrival back at camp, he is greeted with utter chaos: his animals have been stolen by rustlers, his pard Packy Lambert has been killed, and his younger brother Thad is dying with a bullet in his chest . . .